Copyright © 2021 Richard Ireland

All rights reserved. No part of this book or its illustrations may be reproduced in any form or by any electronic or mechanical means, including information storage and retrieval systems, without permission in writing from the publisher, except by reviewers, who may quote brief passages in a review.

ISBN
978-1-716-20474-6

Illustrations and Cover Design by Richard Ireland
Formatting by Jazmine Ireland

Printed in Aberystwyth, Wales, United Kingdom

Published by Lulu

All characters and scenarios are fictitious and used for the purpose of entertainment.

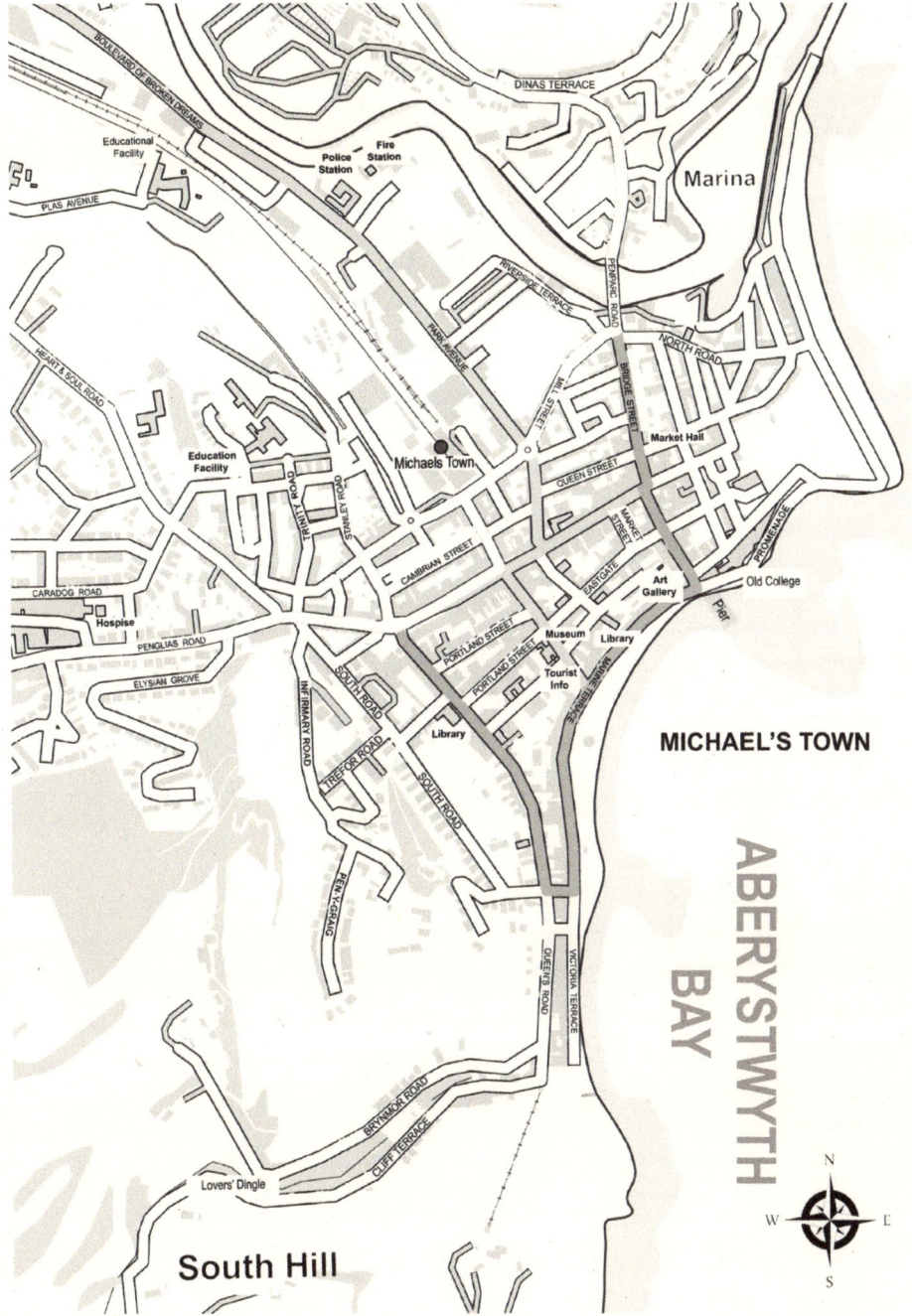

ALL THIS TIME

RICHARD IRELAND

To Mali

For Kanooke (2005 – 2020)
This man's best friend - lost in lockdown.

Contents

LOCK-IN - p. 15

GWYNT Y DDRAIG - p. 36

V.O.O.D.O.O.. MURDER OF CROWS PART I - p. 52

COPYCAT - p. 88

BOTTLE IT - p. 132

V.O.O.D.O.O.. MURDER OF CROWS PART II - p. 158

ALL THIS TIME

LOCK-IN

LOCK-IN

1

"Can I ask you to go through your statement once more before you sign it please." The Detective Inspector slides the paperwork across the table until it disappears out of sight and onto her lap.

"Jesus - how many more times? Look - it took a lot for me to come here in the first place - and of my own volition. Me and my mates made a pact not to say a word, to anybody - but I simply can't live with it any longer - so why would I lie about any of it - you've checked out The Crow's Nest I presume - all the evidence is there for you to see."

My questions were met with silence from the Detective Inspector, her young male colleague sitting next to her and my fish-faced solicitor next to me, so I took a deep breath.

It had only been three weeks, but we were all pissed off with the lockdown - we tried having a night out - at home, but it was crap to say the least. Kids running into the room - a wife asking to turn the music down and a torrent of buzzing or calling mobile phones. We had to get out and meet up - so we decided on The Crow's Nest. It was a no-brainer as the three of us had cut our alcoholic teeth there when we were young teens. Ironically the place had just closed down - about a fortnight before lockdown. The windows were all boarded up and the front door had a massive metal girder bolted and pad locked across it - but we knew the place well enough - and had helped out the old landlord, Gruff, to load the cellar years before. Two of us even had a bit of an argument over who had painted the pub sign as we walked past it. One of us said it was Gruff himself but the other was adamant it had been his brother. We found our way in via the barrel doors - down the dark alleyway at the side of the building - was as easy as it was exciting. We felt like kids again.

"Look at this - everything's all here," says Mickey, gently sliding his hand along the top of a chair and checking it for dust - there was very little.

"Funny smell Irvine?"

"It's stale beer Dennis - that's all - always reminds me of the morning after - you know?"

"On you or her?" Dennis asks cheekily,

"At least I'd know," Irvine smirked proud of his own comeback as he quickly made his way behind the bar - picked up an upturned pint glass, blew into it and placed it under one of the beer pulls attached to the bar. It hissed and spat out what could only be described as dusty foam when pulled. "For fuck-sake!" he exclaimed.

"You didn't actually expect the draught to be on, did you Irvine?" asked Mickey flicking a wink at Dennis. "That's why Dennis had the foresight to bring his own." Dennis pulled out a bottle of Pink Gin from the hessian bag he was carrying.

"I don't want that pink shit!" declared Irvine while he desperately searched through the darkened fridges behind the bar, finishing with a slammed fisted attempt to get into the old till.

"I wouldn't have had one off you anyway - you blew into the glass." Mickey said with sarcastic chastisement towards the back of Irvine's bald head.

"You what?" Irvine appeared angry - which was his most comfortable default setting and not genuine at all. "Oh - you mean all the germs and virus and shit - bollocks - if your time is up - your time is up."

Mickey chuckled, which made Irvine spin around to face the other two at the very moment a chink of glass could be heard as Dennis produced a second bottle from the bag. This time Irvine's favorite - 'Jack Danial's'. Irvine hop-scotched his large and heavy body over to Dennis - who was defenseless - as his hands now gripped two large bottles – to stop Irvine's big handed clamped - forehead - kiss.

"You are - a fuckin' star!" Irvine grunted aggressively. "What you got Mickey boy?"

"Bottles of Bud..." Mickey quickly followed up before Irvine could protest, "and a half bottle of Voders for later." Irvine and Dennis looked at each other and let out a loud but very feminine 'woo,' quickly copied by a self-depredating Mickey.

After some debate online, we had all agreed to stay at the pub overnight - and before you ask if anyone else knew if we were there - no - they didn't. We used the much practiced - oldest one in the book. Each of told, who ever wanted to know, that we were staying with the other for the night, some personal crisis emergency etcetera - while observing social distancing of course. We'd moved the tables and chairs to make a clearing and sat around in a triangle in the middle of the floor.

The leci – sorry electricity - was on so we had 'Guns N' Roses - Appetite for Destruction' playing out of the Jukebox, still the best one in town – and as the drinks flowed, we started singing each track at each other - loud as we could. We knew the volume was behind the bar and had yanked it up above the halfway mark, trust me that's enough. The Crow's Nest is well out the way as you know, so only a Bobby on the beat would have any chance of hearing the music or seeing any slithers of light though the boarded up windows and front door, and since it was shut – and had been for over a month now – we didn't think that a likely scenario.

It was about eleven o'clock when the first one appeared.

"Hay Dennis - you're date's arrived!" Irvine had to shout over the music.

Dennis slowly turned in his seat, not because of Irvine's comment, but the shocked expression he saw on Mickey's face.

"What the f...?"

"Where'd he come from?" Mickey asked Irvine who nonchalantly shrugged his shoulders.

"Where d'you come from pal?" another loud bellow.

The bloke was in a bit of a state. He had a problem standing up straight to start with and was holding his head, which either had dried blood down one temple and onto his cheek – or dirt.

He was in his late twenties I reckon - tattoos on his neck and wearing a T-shirt and jogging bottoms, both soiled with something or other. I would confidently say that, at that point, all three of us thought he was most probably a rough sleeper - who looked like had just woken up.

Irvine repeated his question, this time standing up - the last of the three to do so.

"Hay you want to introduce yourself pal - this is a private function - and you're trespassing," The last track on the Jukebox finished just in time.

"I - was - where am I?" The bloke struggled so Dennis moved over to the other two friends and offered the bloke his seat with a muted arm gesture,

18.

"I was at home," said the stranger. Mickey and Dennis looked at each other - 'That's the rough sleeper theory out of the window then' they collectively thought,

"I was at home with the Missus, then - then - I woke up, down there," he looked around the Pub seemingly taking it in for the first time through painful-looking narrow eyes, "cellar is it?"

"Yah, must have been," said Mickey again looking at Dennis, "No other way in, we must of past him when we came in. He must have been well out-off-it in a dark corner somewhere."

There followed an uncomfortable silence, when all of us looked at each other in turn, hoping the other would pick up on, and answer the telepathic 'what do we do now' question.

"Hey!" Irvine broke the silence and stillness by briskly walking towards the bar where the drinks were neatly lined up, "You look like you could do with a drink, yes?" The bloke nodded lethargically. Irvine took a cheeky look at Dennis as he placed his large hand around the bottle of Pink Gin - but then took it away again and poured out a generous shot of his own Jack Danial's into a new glass before handing it to the stranger. "Keep hold of it now," he said clasping the blokes second hand to the glass, "we don't tolerate any waste or spillages here." The stranger took a very small sip. "Come on man," encouraged Irvine, "there's plenty more where that came from," he gave Dennis another look and a verifying nod – Dennis correctly read it as a request to replenish the alcohol supplies with a trip to the nearest Spar before they closed, so gave a reluctant nod back. The stranger, strained to look up at Irvine's face so high above his own - looked down at the drink, and proceeded to swallow the lot in one go.

"That's the way!" exclaimed Irvine excitedly as he quickly snatched back the glass and moved back to the bar for a re-fill for both himself and the stranger. Dennis stealthfully took Mickey's arm, turned away from the onlooking stranger and lent in close with a whisper.

"Well that's put the kibosh on it!" He nodded with a pout of the lips. "I'm not sticking around here all night with 'Worzel Gummidges' younger brother." The two friends giggled like schoolboys.

Irvine returned from the behind the bar with the drinks, once again handing one to the slumped stranger.

"There you go pal," he turned towards Mickey and Dennis, "More the merrier - right?" That life-long friendship telepathy in play again.

"Now who's got a couple of quid for the Juke - I feel a bit of 'The Strangers' coming on."

"Well actually Irvine - mate," Mickey said, louder than a whisper but low enough to not be heard by the stranger, as he moved closer to Irvine - "we're were thinking about - calling it a night."

"What?" An expected reaction from the big man, "We said all night - we've haven't even got started yet," he pointed at Dennis, "He's still got all his clothes on and he's nowhere near to tears yet!"

"I know - but Irvine this guy..."

"So, what - on a normal night the place would be packed anyway - what difference does it make to anything? Your just worried about the bloody wife giving you grief aren't you - I'm surprised you turned up at all to be honest - just about managed to crawl out from under her bloody thumb!"

"Yah?" Mickeys voice elevates to Irvine's volume, "Well not all of us are sitting at home trying to think up ways to amuse ourselves – some of us have reasonability's towards our families,"

"We're? You mean you - as always. Dennis' Mum's gone to his sisters' place - you're the only one with a wife and kids," Irvine was wide-eyed with a necessary to concentrate when arguing with Mickey.

"Exactly - that's my point - I have an obligation to my wife and kids."

"So did I once upon a time - if your memory serves you Mickey? - You've got to have a life as well you know!"

"And that's why she left you Irvine..." Mickey and Irvine continue arguing until Dennis stops them both with a touch of the arm and a nod towards the seated stranger. They all look at him just before he slides to the side of the chair and falls to the floor with an unsettling thump, his empty glass rolling towards, and stopping at the three friends' feet.

We all instantly went into Medi-emergency mode and scrambled around the stranger - checked his pulse - breathing - eyes etcetera. We all decided that calling for an Ambulance was the right thing to do. The other two had deliberately left their phones behind but I had brought mine along - or so I thought - but after checking my pockets I realized that it was perched on the passenger seat of my car losing battery power by the minute, and my car was tucked away out of sight down the road from the Pub, so one of us had to go and get it.

"Keys - there they are. I'll be back now in a minute." Irvine tried the front door of the Pub which was solidly shut tight. "I'll have to go back through the Cellar."

"They've done a hell of a security job on this place haven't they? Observed Mickey checking out the boarded windows - which must have been inside and out as he had noticed the surprisingly good quality wooden sheet coverings as they arrived.

"How the hell are the Paramedics going to get him out," asked Dennis, "down those old stone steps and through the Cellar - and up to the hatch again. There's no chance - you'd need a Cave Rescue Team for that."

"He's got a point - for once," said Irvine standing tall with arms away from his body - adrenaline obviously playing its part, "I'll get the phone first and foremost - I'll call 999 and give them the low-down on my way back." He left through the small door that led down to the Cellar.

"How's he doing Mickey?" asked Dennis, moving closer to the unconscious stranger for the first time.

"Well he's breathing - just."

"How the hell are we going to explain this one then Mickey? If my work get wind of it - I've had it. 'Senior Council Official Caught in illegal lockdown lock-in," I can see the bloody headline now — what'll my mother say?"

"Don't stress Dennis, when Irvine comes back, I'm going tell him that you need to go back home - we'll keep you out of it." Dennis let's out a massive sigh of relief and with some emotion in his voice, thanks his friend sincerely.

"Hay, you two!" A very loud Irvine re-appeared making Dennis jump, "I can't get out!"

"What d'you mean?" Dennis said, the panic returning in his voice,

"The barrel doors to the Alley are shut solid - I can't get them to open - we're screwed boys!"

"No Irvine," Mickey piped up with one eye on Dennis "we're temporarily stuck - that's all!"

"No, we're not," said Dennis quietly, "we're fucking locked-in!"

We put the stranger into a more comfortable position on the cushioned seat against the wall at the back of the bar and kept an eye on him, in case he moved, also checked on his breathing every ten to fifteen minutes or so. In time we had all had a go at the barrel doors from the Cellar - you could push them upwards enough to see that a padlock had been added since we'd arrived and to make things worse - you could see the keyhole on the base. But with no key - we were indeed - trapped.

"Come on Dennis," Irvine was uncharacteristically softly spoken as he poured his friend another generous measure of Pink Gin, "have another one - there's only a bit left anyway - make you feel better." Dennis threw it down his throat - then brought it all back up again.

2

The next twelve hours or so, were a roller-coaster of exhaustion, panic and confusion. We all played our part in attempting to find a weakness in the unbelievably thorough secure features that had been added to The Crow's Nest after its closure. The electric was still on of course, but no phone signal from the landline - another obvious I know. We tried to look for a screwdriver – we found a lemon slicing knife in one of the drawers behind the bar, but on closer inspection we found the screws were of that type that needed a specific tool - and they were more like bolts than screws anyway. One of us - you can guess who - even tried chucking a chair at one of the boards, but it just bounced off - heavy bloody thing too. No, we were stuck inside for - well as long as it would take for someone to inspect the building or something - and as our second night there approached, we all just sat - looking at each other - in complete - lockdown.

"Look Mickey - he's awake!" Dennis was the first of the friends to speak for some time. The stranger staggered to his feet, Irvine getting up and moving towards him slowly, his hands outstretched ready to catch him if he fell.

"Stay away!" The stranger shouted aggressively, "Who are you people and why did you kidnap me - what you after - huh?" He'd picked up a glass with water in - ready for him if needed in the night - emptied it onto the floor and was holding it like a weapon. Irvine held up his hands in surrender and stopped moving forward.

"We were already here mate - you just turned up - last night from the Cellar, remember?"

"Bullshit!" Barked the stranger, "you're a bunch of nonces or something aren't you?"

"What the hell was that noise?" asked Dennis suddenly.

"Yah, whatever - what d'you think I am?" The stranger was shushed by the others who had all heard a heavy sound coming from behind the Cellar door.

That's when two more blokes came staggering through into the bar. One smartly dressed pushing his way past the other, a much older guy with a big beard and dreadlocks, who collapsed as a result. The smartly dressed one made it to the bar before he keeled over and lay himself out on the floor.

"What's this then?" The stranger asked, after a moment of silence.

"We told you - we don't know," answered Irvine with a fatherly tone, "now put that glass down – cause you're really starting to piss me off - and you don't want to do that."

"He's right," said Mickey, "whatever's going on here - we're all in it together."

"We need to get out of here - now!" Dennis ran to the front door, where he spent some time kicking and hitting it - pointlessly. Mickey went to his aid once he slid down to the floor and started weeping.

24.

3

The stranger still wasn't completely convinced of our innocence until the smartly dressed guy woke up the next morning and reacted in the same way he had, just this time towards him as well as us. The old boy with the dreads never woke up. It was later that day - around six that we again heard the sounds of more disoriented bodies approaching the bar from the cellar. Three this time - all shapes and sizes - and one of them was a woman. I remember, she had bright blue hair and rings on all her fingers that were cut up a bit and completely covered in old blood. The other two guys looked like brothers - and no - not just because they were both Asian - they did actually look a lot alike. We tried to make the soon-to-be unconscious newcomers comfortable - as we knew by now that they weren't coming around till the morning. The old guy with the dreads was dead - nothing we could do, so we put him into the ladies with his own coat over his face.

Yet another night kept in, colder than the previous. The three of us collected water in jugs from the sink in the gents and started to distribute it into glasses from behind the bar, half-hidden behind the big crow sculpture that had always lived there - where we could talk quietly without everybody else listening in.

"Dennis what the hell are you doing?" Asked Irvine, who simply did not have the ability to whisper affectively.

"I'm caressing the crow of course." Dennis answered, rubbing his hand along the heavy, dark sculpture.

"Don't be so bloody stupid – bloody old wives' tale …" Irvine was dismissive of the Pub's mythological superstition that, all will be well if you caress the crow.

"Caress the crow and life will become as the crow flies – straight forward." Dennis was quoting the myth. "Anything's worth a try at this point Irvine, don't you think."

"Bollocks!" Irvine's one-word response prompted Dennis to stop trying.

"I think I've got a plan." Mickey was very careful that only Irvine and Dennis heard him, "There all coming from the cellar, right? So, we go down and wait."

"Wait for what?" Asked Dennis nervously, Irvine answered him.
"We wait to see how they're getting in."

"If they can get in," interrupted Mickey, "then..."

"We can get out!" Dennis was too loud, but it didn't matter. The stranger and the smartly dressed man were lost in their own deep thoughts at the other side of the bar and the rest were still unconscious.

So down we went - one after the other. We didn't say anything to the other two that were conscious - just left them to it - the first guy was a prick anyway – not even a thank you for setting him straight when he collapsed - and the smartly dressed one hadn't said a word the whole time yet – since he accused us all of being his kidnappers that is. If they wondered down to the cellar at some point, then so be it - all we cared about was getting out.

It had seemed to be a nice day outside, but we found an incredibly cold and uncomfortable corner where we could just about make out the sun light through the thin spaces of the heavy metal barrel door. We had tried it again quickly when we first arrived down there - just in case - you know. None of us knew what to expect - the anticipation was a nightmare. The other two had fallen asleep, lent on each other - I had a pounding headache and we were all starving hungry, cold and tired, but all that disappeared when I saw a shadow cut the thin light and heard heavy boots on the metal plate of the door. We helped each other stand silently, we'd been there for about two hours I reckon and were a bit stiff.

"Hay - you - let us out!" I screeched, as I lunged towards the short ladder that lead to freedom - then we saw the door opening and slam down on the ground behind it. I climbed two of the four rungs which put me at eye level with the street outside. A large male figure dressed head to toe in black and wearing a medical looking face-mask, stood looking down at me - spun to the side, as if to pass a rugby ball, and dispatched a limp figure he'd just received from another pair of blacked out arms, through the doorway - behind me - and let fall onto the big plastic coated sponge mat, designed for tumbling barrels, at the others feet. It was another bloke. This time a skinny skinhead with not a stitch of clothes on him. I called out and tried to reason with - whoever - or however many of them there were out there - but they remained silent. A crate full of bottles of beer followed next knocking me back to the ground from the small ladder - the skinhead had luckily rolled aside by now. At the same time, the door hinges creaked and slammed out the light - along with our chances of escape.

"We'll keep these down here." Irvine says as he attempts to pop the cap off the top of one of the beer bottles using the uneven stone wall of the cellar.

"Irvine what are you doing? Just leave it," Mickey puts the bottle back into the crate,

"I'm thirsty,"

"Then drink water Irvine - you know that - better get this one upstairs I suppose." All three agreed but it only took Mickey and Irvine to carry him through - Irvine said he could've carried him on his own - he was so light.

"Dennis run on ahead and grab the dead dreadlock guys coat, will you? This one is bloody freezing." Mickey says.

"What - do I have to?"

"Just don't look at his face," added Irvine.

When we got back up to the bar, the two Asian guys, who looked like brothers, were up and about with their backs to us standing over the still unconscious woman with bright blue hair. They were talking jovially to the smartly dressed guy. None of them took much notice of the skinhead being put to lie on the seat next to them with the dead dreadlocks' coat draped over him - that's when we could see that the closest Asian guy was stacking three - ten-pound notes in his open-palmed hand. He held them there while the smartly dressed guy slid closer in his backwards facing seat with a smirk on his face as the second Asian guy undid his fly and started to take a piss over the bright blue hair in front of him. Before any of us could say anything - she woke up and went nuts! She was very thin - but once she stood up - very tall and feisty. She lashed out at the laughing men.

First, she punched the Asian guy straight at his open fly - then kicked out at the other. The smartly dressed guy stood from his seat - dropped his smile in an instant and told her, very calmly to go on then - if she dare.

"Everybody, just calm down!" Irvine's bellow did the trick. "We're all going to sit," he raised a finger as if to command a dog, "and I'll explain what's going on here - best I can - and when our meeting is concluded I will produce a crate of beer - as a peace offering." Mickey and Dennis were quite impressed - up to the beer part - but now just threw up their heads and eyes at each other as they sat along with their fellow freshly-conscious patrons, who now consisted of; the first guy to appear - the stranger, the smartly dressed guy, the two Asian lads and the blue haired woman - who was still swearing under her breath as she ran her fingers through her wet hair and wiped them on her tight jeans.

"Right," Irvine was loving it, "I'll start from the beginning and tell you all we know."

So, he did, and then sent Dennis down to the cellar to get the crate of beers. Mickey and Dennis declined the offer of a couple of bottles and so did the smartly dressed guy, only not so politely. Irvine divided the crate of twenty-four between the rest, letting the woman have his fifth following a brief but intense protest from her.

The night drew in and the drinking went on - without any incident surprisingly - and for the first time since we had arrived - everyone was chilled out. That was until the smartly dressed guy suddenly spoke up from nowhere and said that it would be easy to get out of here if we wanted. Everyone was hooked and some were restlessly excited.

He said that all we needed to do is crank up the jukebox as loud as it will go, occasionally turn off and on the lights, stack some chairs and tables below the main window and - set them on fire. Most seemed inspired by this and not alarmed at all about the possibility that we would all die of smoke inhalation before any fire could cause enough damage for us to get out - or anyone to notice from outside - on one of the quietest streets in Michael's Town at the best of times - let alone in a lockdown.

"Stop her Irvine for Christ sake!" Dennis pleaded with his friend to stop the woman with blue hair searching through the cabinets and drawers behind the bar for matches, a lighter, paper and or any type of accelerant.

"Will you just stop and think about this for a minute, please!" Mickey had to shout at the top of his voice over the Jukebox - his plea only reaching the smartly dressed guy who was watching, laughing and relishing at the chaos around him from the chair he was sitting in.

She never found anything to start a fire - thank god. The other suggestions were carried out however. The juke was cranked up so high that the 'Hotel California' baseline vibrated through the place with a horrible distortion - someone turned the lights off and on like a strobe for far too long every couple of minutes or so. People were running about screaming and shouting as loud as they could. We didn't get involved - just perched ourselves behind the crow sculpture on the other side of the bar again. The arrival of another four souls from the cellar dulled the proceedings for a minute or two, but they were quickly ignored as they collapsed and the raucous continued.

We put the four new arrivals - all men - into a semi comfortable position to sleep off – what we now agreed, was a forced drugged state. The blue haired woman, Asian lads and the stranger started asking us to line up glasses from behind the bar - it was do it, or they would, so we did it. They threw each glass with such power that the glass almost turned to a glittery dust cloud on impact with the front door and boarded up windows. The floor and tabletops by the main window were quickly receiving a dusting of glistening glass fragments which seemed to continue to emit light when the Pub suddenly went dark and silent.

"Who turned the Jukebox off?" Asked Dennis, who never would have been heard a second before.

"Lights have stayed off too!" Irvine said softly, just for his friends.

"I think they've cut the leci boys!" Announced Mickey.

The electricity stayed off. There was shuffling in the dark as everyone found a seat - and stayed there. The woman with blue hair woke me up - as well as most of the others I suspect - in the middle of the night - it was still dark. She screamed that there was no water in the gents and the toilet only half flushed. So - these guys had cut both the electric and water from outside the building - a result of the ear-splitting demonstration no doubt.

"It can't get any worse - can it Mickey?" Whispered Dennis, his voice even more fragile sounding in the dark.

"It'll be alright mate, once the sun comes up - I've got a plan." Mickey replied. "Try and get some sleep."

4

The next morning was like a scene from a war film - everybody who had drank the beers was ill. Some began with the shits - others vomiting and one managing - involuntarily of course - both at once. The toilet quickly became a 'no go area' so - most people had no option but to be sick - or worse - where they sat, stood or lay. By the time the four new arrivals had woken from their drug induced states, all the rest were semi-conscious, in a fetal position and back on the cushioned seats.

"I can't stand it Irvine," Dennis was talking about the smell. A strange mixture of stale beer and sweet slurry with a dash of pickled onion gas thrown in for measure.

"What's he doing?" Irvine asks his friend,

"Who?"

"Mickey 'Florence Nightingale' over there. He's going from one to the other."

Irvine raised his voice. "Stay away Mickey mate - social distancing - remember."

"They're really ill actually Irvine - completely dehydrated and some are delusional," Mickey shouted back with concerned concentration on his face, "I think they've been poisoned!"

"What?" Dennis checked the floor by his feet to make sure he was still standing in a dry patch while Mickey rejoined them both behind the bar.

"Irvine how come you're alright?" Mickey asked, the three standing as if a sporting prep talk was taking place,

"I did have the shits first thing this morning, but that's all - nothing else - I'm fine. Mind you, I only had two and half bottles - couldn't be arsed - or able to find the rest - after the lights went out, didn't want to drink anyone else's by mistake ... covid and all that."

30.

"Where did you go? Not in that toilet." Dennis pulled a face of disgust,

"I went in the ladies didn't I," Irvine said quite proudly,
"With the dead Dreads guy?"

"Yah?" Irvine replied with a 'so what' tone.

"Look you two," Mickey leaned in closer to Dennis and Irvine taking each of them by the arm to grab their attention, "Those beers were intended to be found by..." he counted on his fingers, "seven people - and that's including the skinhead, they arrived with."

"What about it?" Irvine wasn't following,

Dennis intervened.

"They must have known the skinhead would be in no fit state to drink," his mental wheels were turning as he spoke, "so it's actually more like six."

" Exactly!" Mickey started to clarify for Irvine's sake. "Twenty-four divided by six equals..."

"Four!" Exclaimed Dennis with no delay.

"That can't be right. I dished out five each - I had four because of that gnarly cow kicking up such a fuss," questioned Irvine.

"You weren't meant to have any," Mickey continued to try and clarify, "we're not supposed to be here. So minus us three, there was; one, the stranger," he counted on his fingers again - this time for the benefit of his friends, "two, the smartly dressed guy, three, the old guy with the dreads - deceased - but they don't know that - four and five, the Asian brothers and six, the blue haired Woman. Forget the skinhead - they knew he was out of it until the next day." Mickey raised a finger quickly to stop any interruption from Irvine, "But as it happened – you, Irvine, were included but Dennis, me and the smartly dressed guy declined the offer - and of course, we're alright," they all looked over at the smartly dressed guy, who was asleep in a chair, "at least I think we all are."

"So, what you're saying is," Dennis was now in clarification mode, but finished with hysteria "our captors are trying to poison us all!"

"Calm down you noisy basted," hushed Irvine impatiently as Mickey squeezed on their arms a little harder and moved in even closer. "That's not all. When I was going around - seeing how everyone was doing - a couple of them were mumbling apologies and pleading for mercy,"

"Who?" asked Irvine,

"The woman with blue hair said, 'she didn't mean to do it - and she loved her kids. And the stranger said that it wasn't his fault - that she had driven him to it."

"Shit Mickey, the penny had dropped for Irvine and the Pubs lights came back on, "what did the Asian lads say?"

"I don't know?" Mickey looked puzzled at the question.

So we - rightfully - came to the conclusion that all the patrons, dead or alive, were abusers in one way or another - but we weren't – that's when we came up with the idea of a note - for our captors - appeal to their sense of fair justice - after all they were obviously some sort of vigilante group - probably using police scanners - or just word on the street - to track down, drug, kidnap, imprison and ultimately poison their victims - or perpetrators - depends on how you look at it I suppose.

"Our names are Irvine, Mickey and Dennis. We were already in the building before you sent the first abuser in and locked the barrel doors. We are innocent. Please reply to this note and leave it here in the cellar. All we want is to get out of here and return back to our families - we will say nothing." Mickey looks up at Dennis and Irvine, "What do you think?"

Both the other two agree that it's good and straight to the point. Mickey folds the note - written on the back of a cocktail price list then slides it back into a plastic sleeve - and slips off down to the cellar where he will leave it sticking out of the gap next to the padlock in the barrel doors.

It was getting late that night when we heard movement from the cellar. One of the last lot - the four souls – used to be a local at the Crow's Nest - we knew him well, Bam-Bam we used to call him, cause he used to bang twice on the bar when he wanted another drink. Used to drive the barmaids nuts. Getting away from him and down the cellar was proving to be a bit tricky. That was until the next lot arrived, of course – one of yours one of them - complete with uniform and all - that's right – Policeman, or officer these days, isn't it?

Anyway, the other two enlisted Bam-Bam's help in dealing with three more drugged up abusers while I slipped away to see if we'd had a reply to our note.

Mickey, Dennis and Irvine each read the note found in the cellar, once Bam-Bam had fallen asleep,

'14 WOMEN + 2 CHILDREN KILLED IN THE FIRST 3 WEEKS OF LOCKDOWN.' Mickey counted his fingers once more as he read first, "That's potentially one, for everyone here!" 'IN ORDER TO BE GRANTED RELEASE - YOU MUST ADMINISTER THE FOOD WHICH WILL BE SUPPLIED TOMORROW AT 11:00AM - ALL MUST HAVE AN EQUAL PORTION AND FINISH IT. ONCE COMPLETED - COME TO THE CELLAR AND YOU WILL BE RELEASED. THE CHOICE IS YOURS.'

"Holly shit, they're going to try and poison them again!" Dennis - the last to read the note - was hushed again by Irvine.

"What about it? I mean we don't know that it's poisoned do we - all we do is make sure they all get some food and not have any ourselves - right?"

"But Irvine," Mickey added calmly, "it might look a bit odd if we don't - at least pretend - to eat the food - we are all starving - and most of them are still sick, they might not want any."

"Well," Dennis butted in, "we'll just have to convince them that it's for the best then, won't we - cause I'm getting out of this hell hole no matter what." Dennis checked under his shoe for signs of vomit or faeces.

5

"The note was such a relief to all three of us. They could obviously see that keeping us captive along with these repugnant people was a mistake. So, I'm telling you - for what must be the umpteenth time. We met with the masked captors - took the Curry and Rice upstairs for the others - and while they were tucking in - snuck back through the cellar and were allowed out. That's it - we were free."

The interview room door was knocked quickly, and a handful of documents delivered to the Detective Inspector by a uniformed W.P.C. The D.I. paused and slid a page in front of the young male colleague next to her and what looked like a copy of the same towards the fish-faced solicitor.

"I can go now - right?"

"Wrong - I'm afraid you are under arrest for breaking and entering - houses not the Crow's Nest Pub - assault, kidnap and thirteen counts of causing death by poison. You have the right to remain silent - but anything you do say may be used against you - your legal representative will inform you of your rights."

"But I told you - we were just innocent pawns - I came here of my own free will for Christ sake!"

"Ok - then why can't we find the note; the so-called captors gave you - and more importantly - please explain why..." She lifted her copy of the document into the air, "your fingerprints were found on the padlock used to secure the door."

"Bloody hell - is that all you got - we left via the barrel doors, you stupid copper - I must have grabbed the lock on the way out - I really don't think I would remember a small detail like that - do you?"

"No - understood - but you do remember never approaching the front of the Pub - don't you?"

"That's right - I never did,"

"The prints were found on the padlock securing the front door of the Crow's Nest Pub." Silence.

"Nothing to say?" The D.I. gestured to a uniformed colleague. "Take him down - it's very likely that you will remain in lockdown for the rest of your life sir!"

END

ALL THIS TIME

GWYNT Y DDRAIG

GWYNT Y DDRAIG
(The Dragon's Wind)

UN (1)

Old Tân y Ddraig Farm always gives you that smell in the spring. The smells of pine trees and damp earth with just a little sulphur - beautiful. Empty now of course, a shell of its former glory. It belonged to my brother, Gethin and his wife, Erin - she had Irish blood in her - both dead, along with pour Gwyneth their beloved daughter - lame for the entirety of her short ten- year life. My brother's son Emyr inherited but decided to rebuild from scratch, a field away from Tân y Ddraig, his pride and joy - Fferm Newydd. Stubborn as a mule with the temper of a bull - that's Emyr - caused him to lose his marriage it did. Ceri - lovely looking girl - she lives and works in the City now as a solicitor no less - worked her way up from legal secretary - never looked happy since the divorce though, probably got something to do with not seeing Cai so much anymore - he's the boy - ten going on fifty sometimes - reminds me of his Grandfather, my brother. That is apart from that bit of softness that they all seem to have these days - all that hugging and dancing and internet rubbish - read a book now and then - I've told him that. Cai wants to be a celebrity chef, not just a chef mind – a celebrity with it. Since lockdown Cai sends me little letters - more like notes really. It's very kind of him I know, and I am grateful - but it's that softness again - he should be helping his father on the farm - not troubling himself with 'vulnerables' like me. The government are giving me a food box every week - very nice too – all the good stuff mind. I don't know how he does it - but the notes from Cai arrive attached to it every week.

Dear Great Uncle Gruff,

I hope you are not ill. If you are, give me or Dad a ring and we'll take you to the Hospital. Dad had to pour loads and loads of the milk away today because the big Coffee shops are closed and no one else wants it. He says this will be the end of us at Fferm Newydd. I told him. I said it's alright because all the patients in the Hospitals will need loads of milk cause it helps to make them strong again.

I'll send you another note next week.

P.S. You can send me one back if you like. Tell me and I'll come down on my bike and pick it up from outside the house.

Lots of love, Cai XXX.

Wish he had left the kisses out. Emyr - Cai's Father - would say to me 'Dairy's the only way forward Gruff' (pronounced 'Griff') - short for Gruffudd - that's me. I live in the town, never was the farming type - my life lead down another path a long time ago - but that's another story.

DAU (2)

The pretty landscape looked sad - the grasses and cattle bowing their heads with every breeze - as the sun shuts its eyes for a time behind an awesome cloud the colour of dirty dish water. I have walked up the hill from town, it's not very far but takes it out of me a bit, so I sit on the largest quartz rock in a cluster of three and prepare my pipe for lighting. I can see both farms from here - new and old - I look mostly at the old. It used to be full of crops - ten acres I think - surrounding the main house. Wild horses would frolic and suddenly gallop off over the horizon together – and then, there was the welsh wall. The wall faced the main road - the wall my brother decided to paint a giant Welsh flag on. It was spectacular - especially in its infancy. A boring old red brick wall used for god knows what in the past - must have been twelve-foot-high and twenty wide. Gethin - my brother - had painted the whole thing white, then found some green paint for the bottom half and must have gone off and bought the red. It was such a bright red everyone could see it clearly from the road - in fact in the summer we would always get the odd tourist couple driving up the drive from the main road thinking we were a museum or cafe of some sort - bloody idiots. We all teased Gethin -after he'd applied the green - saying that's the easy bit - you'll never manage the dragon - it's too complicated - because it is, take a good look next time. A month - one summer - it took him. At night he would use the light from the tractor and sit up there on some scaffold like Michelangelo with the smallest of brushes, face almost pressed up against the wall he was painting. My mother would ask us 'where's your brother gone to now?' 'Up the wall' everybody else would reply. I'll never forget the day it was finished. Gethin would hang tarpaulin down from the scaffold the closer to completion it got. On this day he gathered the whole family to stand in front, the scaffold had gone but the tarp remained - that is until he pulled one side and there it was. Truly magnificent it was too. My grandmother even swore in welsh and was told off by my mother.

The wall stands about two-foot-tall now, the hint of a red claw with about forty percent red brick showing through the remains of white and green paint. The house was not much better - although you could still make out the partition walls and there was still the old sink in the kitchen with copper pipes sticking out from it as if it had been slain by a matador. Emyr's new dairy farm - Fferm Newydd - looked eerily quiet. Last time I was up here I saw lads down there, sweeping the yards, mucking out, moving the cows from field to milking shed and back again - but now there was nothing. Emyr had let the two boys go well before lockdown, Brexit was the villain that time. He sold a percentage of his cattle I believe and was talking about converting a couple of barns to offer them out as some sort of 'Luxury Accommodation Farming Experience', all the rage apparently.

Looks like progress on that front was slow too, judging by the pile of new timber outside one of the barns, yet to be touched. There are dandelion seeds everywhere you look - noticed that on the walk up here as well - and the seeds are flying through the air making my hair itch and appearing to evaporate as they stray above my lit pipe.

Poor Cai - I'll get him something - something a boy should have - something of sheer fun. I'll get him a gun - the biggest in the shop. Helen - my neighbour - will get it for me. She's always asking if I need anything from the shop - usually it's just some more pasta to go with the colossal amount of tinned tomatoes they put in those food boxes,
but this time I'll ask her to get me the Gun.

Dear Great Uncle Gruff,
              Wow… the TS-R Norf Super Soaker is soooo… cooool.

Thank you sooooo… much.

I will play with it at the old farm like you said you used to in your note.
 Dad shouted at someone on the phone yesterday and has been in a funny mood ever since and even when Mr. & Missus Forsyth from the Forsyth's Hotel in town came round, he was not at all polite, I had to offer them Tea and biscuits cause I hadn't made any cake yet.

Anyway, I love the TS-R Norf Super Soaker but not as much as I love you,

Lots of love, Cai XXX.

Jesus - the Forsyth's, what the hell are they doing up there? I bet they'll going to buy him out - Christ - they own most of the bloody town already. Forsyth's Hotel - Forsyth's Fish & Chip Shops - Forsyth's Sportswear, even Forsyth's bloody Sex Shop - but it isn't called Forsyth's - Nut's N' Knots, I think, I wouldn't know. And I'll be having words with that Helen too - bloody water pistol - I mean get the boy something that shoots those sticky-sucky things at least. Twenty quid that was. I wish I could get to see Emyr - although - it's nothing to do with me - I have been told that before. Bloody lockdown - bloody Forsyth's - bloody hell!

TRI (3)

Dear Great Uncle Gruff,

It's really late 00:12 on my clock, but I've got to tell you what happened today at the old farm. I didn't have any empty food cans like you said in your note that you gave me with the TS-R Norf Super Soaker because I put them all out for recycling the other day, so I started shooting at the tree that looks like it has Army Camouflage all over it, and something really weird happened. It glowed red for a second and when I sprayed it again, up in the branches, it glowed for a bit longer that time and it was fire cause I could feel it on my cheeks and when it stopped there was a bit of smoke. I smelt the water in the gun in case it was petrol or something, but it wasn't. So, I tried again, this time on some stones and it happened again. The stones glowed with red hot sparkles. I went to do it on a line of bricks on the floor but tripped backwards when I shot it. The water in the air made shapes, out of fire. I did it a couple more times and I swear I could see, horses with long manes in the sky. I kept pumping more and more water into the sky above the bricks but stopped when I saw a giant Dragons face, it was scary. Did that happen to you when you used your Super Soaker in the old farm?

So, I told Dad about it but all he wanted to do was sit down with a cup of Tea and talk about other things. He said that he didn't think he could keep his promise to send me to Michel Roux Jr's Sauce by The Langham cookery school when I turned twelve. But I told him that it was alright (I didn't tell him that Mum had already said she would pay for it - and take me there - but that was two years away yet anyway). Then he was going on for ages about how he should have listened to you and Tadcu Gethin (did he like to cook - cause you said he was like me?) and not been so ambitious, trying to modernize everything.

Anyway, I might not go back to the old farm tomorrow, give it a rest for a while. But when lockdown is over me and you can go there together and make the fire happen again. If you bring your Super Soaker, we can make it even bigger cause I'll feel braver with you there.

Lots of love, Cai XXX.

"Hello - Emyr?"

"Hello Gruff, well there's a surprise, you, using the phone. How are you? Cabin fever set in yet?"

"Well I can't complain really - apart from the police getting in touch with me this morning."

"Oh - what about?"

"I not sure really – some sort of incident at the pub, they wouldn't say what. Just asking about the last time I was at The Crow's Nest and whether I thought it was amply secured or not when I'd left. I told them that I had my leaving do weeks ago and the Brewery had overseen all that stuff since."

"Board kids or bloody squatters it will be - don't worry about it Gruff."

"I won't - at least I've got a nice garden to sit in when the weather's like today - and that moody sod from next door has stopped coming outside - so I can sit out there in peace and quiet."

"Noisy neighbour, is he?"

"No - it's just an ongoing dispute concerning a bush that's apparently blocking his light - it's nothing. How's business?"

"You never ask me that Gruff - I'm guessing Cai told you. You've learned how to use the internet as well as the phone have you?"

"No - he's been sending me notes with the food parcels I get."

"Oh yes - he volunteers to help pack them every Wednesday at the Church Hall, he said you had one - been putting extra tomatoes in because he knows you like them - good for the prostate he said, you'd said. Did make me laugh - I'm sure he doesn't know what the prostate is. He's a good boy really."

"Yes - Emyr he is - and he's worried about you - and Fferm Newydd. Look tell me to bugger off and mind my own business - but what's going on up there - why are the Forsyth's involved?"

"Oh Gruff - it was all okay you know? Mind we were never big enough to turn a tidy profit - and with sodding Brexit kicking in at the end of the year - those European subsidies due to dry up faster than the Cattle - and now this.

We had a nice little contract with one of the big coffee shop chains, throughout Cloverdragon and due to expand to the mainland in the new year - like to be able to say, 'locally sourced' on the chalkboard lists you know? But since they've closed - that's it - down the drain with it - all of it - sodding sacrilegious - it is."

"What have the Forsyth's got to do with it? They're a canny bunch that lot - sell you a burger and chips for eight quid because they call the bugger a steaklet."

"They want to buy - I'm sure you guessed that. Seventy-five-thousand - and the sheer front of the man - old man Forsyth I mean - even told me that it was grant money from the government. Three different businesses rated at twenty-five-thousand a pop - money for old rope, or new farm property as he put it."

"It's got to be worth at least three times that Emyr,"

"I'm sure it is Gruff - never got it valued and can't at the moment of course. They said, me and Cai can stay on here for up to a year but want an answer in the next three weeks."

"Have you got one for them?"

"Well I didn't think so - until yesterday when I found myself filling in an online application for BetterBuy - you know, the supermarket - they're recruiting lots of extra workers at the moment."

"Does Cai know this?"

"No not yet - I'm going to talk to him tonight. His mother wants him to stay with her for a while,"

"In the City?"

"Yes, I told her what was going on last night - I'd had a few drinks - got a bit emotional - so she thinks I'm depressed and can't allow it to effect Cai - he's delicate she says - it's about the well-being of the boy she says - and she's probably right, she usually is."

"I wish there was more I could do Emyr,"

"So do I, Uncle Gruff - and I do appreciate the call I know you don't like these modern contraptions - and I won't tell you to bugger off either."

"Okay - and look don't bollock the boy for telling me - he's brighter than you think - you should talk to him - and give me a ring - anytime - if you want to talk."

"I will Gruff - thanks - bye."

"See you - Emyr."

PEDWAR (4)

From my garden I can see the setting sun breaking through the distant tree branches - glowing with the luminosity of the brightest embers in wood on a fire. The glow of the setting sun behind me widens my eyes as it lights up the foliage in front of me. The smoke from my tobacco twisting in a slow-motion dance - first blooming - then dissipating like a drop of Indian ink in a glass of water. With the exception, of the last birds bidding the sun a good night, all was silent. There - at that moment - I could have been the last man on earth. I sat, letting the damp of evening creep up my legs until I felt it between me and the chair. No letter from Cai yet. Then a lurching feeling in my lower abdomen followed by a tremendous sense of foreboding.

That's when I heard the sirens - one after the other - two different types, screaming up the hill and out of town, a rare occurrence around here. I hurried inside and felt an involuntary compulsion to ring Emyr up at the farm. The phone rang - and rang - and then fizzled out - quite suddenly like a lifeboat match. All night I tried telling myself that it was nothing, probably a car crash or something, but I couldn't help thinking that Emyr could well have put a match to the new place - claim on insurance maybe. There was nothing I could do, it was already dark. Once the food parcel arrives tomorrow, I'll get myself back up that hill and find out what Emyr is up to. Bloody rules or not!

PUMP (5)

The land was unkempt on the green outside the front of my house. Daisy's, erotic purple coloured clover flowers, cuckoo flowers and buttercups had replaced the dandelion seeds. The ultra-fine dew exposing hundreds of spider-web-hammocks hanging low in-between the most successful of wild flowers and grass. It's a lovely morning, the night has been long. I'm in my sitting room looking out for the food delivery so I can scoot up to the farm straight after. It arrives soon enough and surprisingly has a large envelope attached with my name in Cai's writing.

Dear Great Uncle Gruff,

O.M.G. you won't believe what's happened. Dad wanted to phone you but I said no, let it be a surprise. So, the old farm, Tân y Ddraig, is back!

SURPRISE!

It all started when I was trying to phone Dad from Mums apartment in Jacqui's Town. There was no answer all the time. I tried about 50 times I reckon, anyway Mum had to work so I decided I had to come back and check on Dad. I had a funny feeling in my tummy and everything. So I got on the Transcambrian Bus, using some of the money that Dad gave me and got off (after ages and ages) once I saw the main road that I recognized it. It was getting dark now and there were no lights on at home. I popped in quickly and shouted 'Dad' but he wasn't there. Somehow, I knew he'd gone up to the old farm, so I grabbed my Super Soaker (don't know why, but thanks again) and ran up there.

I found him sitting on a pile of bricks. He was crying and had been drinking Whiskey and he had the shotgun with him. I think he was going to shoot himself in the head.

I put my arm around him and told him everything will be alright and that I didn't want him to shoot himself (which made me want to cry when I said it). Then I thought, yes, and showed him what the water did when you shoot it at stuff in the old farm. It was better than before because it was dark outside now, so the fire lit up really bright like on bonfire night. Dad couldn't believe it at first and through away the whiskey bottle, then he pointed the shotgun at me and said I wasn't really there, just in his head he said. I laughed and called him a silly. Then after a minute he threw the shotgun away and gave me a big squeezy hug. And cried again for a bit. I cried a bit too, don't know why though. Then Dad said 'give me a go' so he shot loads of water into the air and we could see the horses with the long mains again.

46.

Then it was my turn and he had used up all the water, cheek I thought. Then Dad said, 'come with me' and pulled me along quite hard. We went back down the hill and got in the Tractor, it had the slurry tank on the back ready to stink up the place. So, Dad drove back up to Tân y Ddraig and started spraying the whole place as he went around in a big circle.

It was amazing Uncle Gruff! First, we saw the horses, then there were men in baggy shirts and braces with flat caps on working. The fire was getting pretty hot when the horses begun running around us in a circle and me and Dad started laughing a very lot, don't know why? Then we saw the walls starting to climb up higher and higher and the fire somehow made the bricks and roofs come back. It wasn't so hot anymore and we had stopped laughing, that's when the Dragon came. I grabbed onto Dads arm, but he said 'don't be afraid' so I wasn't (I was really). He kept saying 'this is a sign my boy, this is a sign!' The Dragons head came up from the middle of the circle we were making, it was MASSIVE! Then it stood up high in the sky and when it unfolded its even more MASSIVE wings I couldn't breathe for a minute and wanted to cry (don't know why). Then, just like that the horses went in a straight line down the hill to Fferm Newydd and set it on FIRE when they got close to it and started running round it. Dad looked shocked and wanted to stop them, but I said this time, 'it's alright dad, it doesn't matter', then I pointed to the old farm which was now nearly new again. The MASSIVE Dragon was flying up high in the sky, I felt it flying around before I saw it cause it was dark up there. Then it swooped down, we thought it was going to take our heads off, flew around again and then breathed really hot fire onto the only wall that wasn't finished.

The flames came back towards the Dragon as the wall was building and I thought it would burn, but it didn't it just started shrinking and shrinking, swarmed around a bit and then seemed to get sucked into the wall. It all went dark then, and quiet once Dad turned off the Tractor and it smelt like bonfire night then.

My hand hurts now so I can't write any more. This is the longest letter I have ever written. Dad says he will come and pick you up tomorrow with a mask and gloves and bring you up to see the new Tân y Ddraig, the way it was when you and Tadcu Gethin were my age he says.

Lots of love, Cai XXX.

P.S. you won't need to bring your Super Soaker now, unless you want to.

My pipe rattled as it hit the large quartz rock at my feet from my open mouth. There it was - I tried to say those words out loud but my voice quivered too much. There was Tân y Ddraig - dearest old Tân y Ddraig Farm - my home. I hadn't even noticed that Fferm Newydd had completely disappeared - there even seemed to be grass now where it had stood.

I looked away then back just to check I wasn't hallucinating. It was like being back in time. I had stood here, on this very spot so many times before, good and bad, and looked down on this picturesque scene. If I never got to see it again after today - that would be fine - I could not feel more complete. I looked down at my hand, made a fist and released, wondering for a moment - am I dead. Tears raced down my face for the first time in over thirty years.

For the duration of the long slog-of-a-walk up here, thoughts were rushing through my mind. Had Emyr torched the place? Is Cai having some sort of juvenile nervous breakdown? But never - in all my own imagination – would I have believed, but I should of. This place was always special and dare I say, *magical*.

I'll go back home - let them pick me up later - I know Cai would be disappointed otherwise. All his doing this - come to think of it - probably couldn't have happened without him. He's special – like my dear old brother - Gethin.

Right, where's my bloody pipe. Better go or I won't be back in time for Emyr to pick me up - and anyway that fool next door wants to talk to me about something - better not be about that sodding bush again - he tried when I left the house earlier, but I told him I couldn't stop - family emergency.

One more look first.

CHWECH (6)

It was a beautifully hot day, the sunshine kissing all the colours awake. Emyr greets - a very shocked looking - Mr. and - confused looking - Mrs. Forsyth from an old tractor, the renewed Tân y Ddraig Farm a picture postcard backdrop behind him.

"Get in, I'll take you both on a tour," he says. The old couple look at each other and except.

"I was sorry to hear about old Gruff, Emyr. He was a good old sort, but that was a bad business," said Mr. Forsyth as his wife and Emyr helped his overindulgent frame into a small trailer attached to the back of the tractor.

"Yes," said Emyr, the smile dropping from his face, "it was, but all things happen for a reason. That's what Gruff would've said, even that."

The old 'Little grey Fergie' chugged along at a good pace, ensuring a pretty uncomfortable ride for the Forsyth's in the trailer behind. Emyr points out the fully-grown acres of crops that are laid out like a blanket all the way to the horizon where three large white quartz rocks glistened in the streaming sunshine. People were in each field - meters apart and masked - harvesting the ripe and checking the yet to mature. As the tractor continued along the closest crop field, Emyr gave a large wave to his ex-wife Ceri, who was helping to manage the volunteers. She gave him back the sort of smile that indicated reconciliation - and maybe more. One of the volunteers offers her a Cider, to help cool her down in the heat, but she politely declines.

"I'll be having a cup of Tea now in a minute, at the farmhouse, that'll do me fine thanks," Emyr could just make her out to say.

The Forsyth's now start pointing at the welsh wall, the wall painted so long ago with the image of the welsh national flag and looking bright and as colourful as anything in nature - it was back - where it belonged.
They reach the large farmhouse where Emyr stops the noisy tractor and helps his guests out from the trailer. Mr. Forsyth dusts himself down with a huff, but Mrs. Forsyth loved every minute of it, she'd said to Emyr as she re-straightened her summer hat. Another look towards Emyr from Ceri as she turned up on foot from another direction.

"Please come in and join us for Tea and maybe if we're lucky - some cake." She said not stopping before walking past the couple and into the house. Inside was Cai, standing proudly in his apron which reached the floor, and behind a table which had an array of cakes, dainty sandwiches and two large tea pots ready to go.

"I don't know how you did it in three weeks Emyr, but you've transformed this place, but where are the two large barns, I saw here last time?" Asked Mr. Forsyth, sticking to the Tea as he was in business mode.

"They had to go," said Emyr with a smirk, "they didn't fit in with the aesthetics," he looked at Cai, who was looking back at his father, "that we always wanted."

"Well," Mr. Forsyth sat up straight and adjusted his trouser belt from underneath his oversized belly, "I can only surmise that all this work is an attempt to increase the offered price Emyr, am I right - or am I right." He raises his hand as Emyr opens his mouth to speak, silencing him. "So, I'll cut to the quick - one offer - non-negotiable. Two-fifty for the lot!"

Emyr waited for confirmation of permission to speak, and quietly said.

"No."

The discussion went on for a little time with Mr. Forsyth constantly repeating 'quarter of a million', and Emyr replying with a delighted 'no' every time.
The men only stopped once Cai's laughter had got to a volume that they had all noticed.

"These sandwiches and cakes are absolutely divine!" Piped up Mrs. Forsyth with a mouthful, try this Cedric."

"For god sake woman, can't you see I'm trying to..."

Mrs. Forsyth shut her husband up with a fish fingered sized paprika-chicken and date with black truffle oil sandwich slice.

"Bloody hell," he mumbled after a few seconds of chewing, then fell silent until he had finished. Mr. Forsyth looked down at the table as if to look for more, "Where did you get this spread Emyr, you must tell me!"

"My son - Cai made it - all of it - from scratch," said Emyr proudly.

50.

"He's going to be the next big thing, aren't you Cai?" Cai nodded confidently back at his Mother. "The trick is to roast the Paprika in bacon fat, then add the chicken," Cai would've continued but Mr. Forsyth interrupted uninterested in the cooking method.

"How much will you charge, per person, for a spread like this boy?"

Cai started to count with his fingers, he stopped at three and looked at his father, who flashed both hands wide and one hand again.
"Fifteen pounds?" Cai said with less confidence and one eye on his father in case he had got it wrong. But judging by Emyr's smile, he hadn't.
Mr. Forsyth was pulled towards his wife's mouth, still housing food, this time a slice of Sicilian lemon drizzle cake with crystallized ginger topping and a Limoncello centre. She whispered to him and he mumbled to himself until he announced that they would take it.

"Can you manage covers of twenty - twice a week in winter - and four times a week in the summer months?" Mr. Forsyth took another sliced sandwich.

"Yes, but the price goes up five pounds a head for weddings and wakes - and I want it in the form of a contract – signed please."
Emyr and Ceri are astonished with Cai's response.

"Done!" announces Mr. Forsyth who then stands and shakes the little man's hand. Everyone else starts shaking hands with each other, apart from Mrs. Forsyth whose hands are too messy.

"Where'd that one come from Cai?" asked Emyr quietly as both him and Ceri give their son a congratulatory hug.

"Keith Floyd book!" whispered Cai.

The family joined the visitors at the table, sampling all the delights that Cai had created. Cai looked away for a moment down the hall into the sitting room and gazed at the Super Soaker above the fireplace mounted where once the shotgun had sat. His eyes then moved just below it where, propped up in a dark wooden frame was a photograph of a very young Great Uncle Gruff and his brother Gethin, standing together in front of the freshly painted welsh wall at Tân y Ddraig Farm.

END

ALL THIS TIME

V.O.O.D.O.O.
MURDER OF CROWS (PART I)

V.O.O.D.O.O.:
MURDER OF CROWS
PART I

PROLOGE

Veteran Royal correspondent Robyn Wright, who has a holiday home where he was born, in the small coastal town of Michael's Town, on the island of Cloverdragon, wonders why for the third time in a row the Market Hall lease holders chose to close the day the Prince of Wales visited the town.

Whilst on a break from London he decides to investigate. He always wanted to be an investigative journalist but seemed to lack the essential ruthlessness required for the job. Praising the ups and softening the downs of the ever-ongoing saga, that is the British Royal Family, seemed to fit his temperament perfectly.

He has since discovered that the six independent businesses that currently hold stalls at the small Market Hall also refused an invitation to join the local trader's guild, turned down a European rejuvenation grant to improve and expand the building and even declined an offer of a mini-series being filmed over the course of six months called 'The Market'. Traders would have received £750 per week for their trouble.
Robyn looks over his latest page of handwritten research notes.

Some years ago, there was an investigation by the local Police into activity in the Market Hall involving suspected drug deals. It was quickly stopped by the powers that be, an old ex-detective inspector, whom would like to remain anonymous told me that 'They had a man on the inside apparently', but he never knew of any case shut down so fast before, with no convictions or even a report filed.

The local Council, which is the landlord of the Market Hall, refused to comment on any allegations, stating only that they 'will continue to support any small businesses in the town as much as they can'.
Something is going on in there.
Is it criminal?
Was there some sort of cover-up?
Does it involve all six stall holders? Two stalls are vacant, and have been for some time apparently (used for storage) why?
Are there not new prospective enterprises waiting for or applying for a stall.
(Note: Contact Council with the premises to rent a stall - see what they say.)

Not wanting to introduce myself yet, I sent a request, by post to each stallholder, stressing that any information given will be treated with the utmost confidentiality.

One replied.

    Robyn waits at a coffee shop on the promenade for a secret meeting with one of the Michael's Town market traders whom has been in touch and wants to remain anonymous.
He sits up and checks his hair with his hands once he sees a very attractive woman enter and sit at the table with him. She smiles.
    'Hello, thank you so much for coming, what will you have?' He says politely.
A waiter of Arabic origin instantly appears and takes their drinks order.
    'Sorry, I'm Robyn. What shall I call you?'
    'You can use my name, Delilah.' She reaches for her mobile phone, while Robyn stares at the cool illuminating light taking nothing away from her subtly made up face. He sees a picture of a Jack Russell on the home screen before it goes blank once laid down on the table.
    'Cute dog, I've got one myself.'

'Jack - unoriginal I know, but he was a rescue pup.'

'That's lovely and if I may say so, very commendable. Would you believe - mines Russell'. He laughs nervously. 'I can tell you are a very loving person.'

'You can?' She replies with seductive eyes and another smile.

'Yes, it's all part of my job. I know I'm chief Royal correspondent, but my true calling has always been investigative journalism. I've got a certain nose for it.'

'A very nice nose it is too.'
Robyn excepts the compliment but seems distractedly uncomfortable and is unsuccessful at concealing it.

'Lot more crows in the garden this year, a whole flock of them this morning. Someone said it means there's trouble brewing from the east.'

'It's murder,' Delilah says, calming taking another drink.

'What?'

'A group of crows is known as a murder.'

'Oh - yes - I knew that. I thought there for a moment that you were about to give me a scoop,' Robyn let out a pathetic fake laugh.

'What do you wish to know Mr. Wright?'

'Robyn, please.' He missed the fact that he had not used his surname when introducing himself. Delilah, through him a smirk and glanced at his untouched drink.

'Don't you like it Robyn?'

'Oh yes.' he took a drink. 'Very nice. What's going on at the Market Hall Delilah - and why do the lease holders continue to opt out of any activities or promotional possibilities without good reason?'
He sat back, looking pleased with the directness of his well-rehearsed question but almost out of breath from it.
Delilah took an extra one before she spoke.

'All six traders at the Market Hall are part of a top secret, highly trained, government funded auxiliary unit specializing in sabotage and assassination - It's known as V.O.O.D.O.O. - Voodoo.'

Robyn wrote nothing with the poised pen in his hand and just looked dead ahead at Delilah, who continued.

'And yes, all the clichés do apply. Fighting in the shadows with a cloak and dagger. Secret missions and special skills, a license to kill, but often left out in the cold.'

Delilah could see a thin sheen of sweat on Robyn's brow.

'You OK, Robyn?'

'I ... I... I just, I feel a little dizzy.'

Delilah unbuttoned her blouse twice.

'It is very stuffy in here, and too many people for comfort - let's go outside - I know just the place to reveal more, if you wish?'

Robyn agreed with a nervous nod.

Delilah suggests taking the cliff railway up to the coastal path at the top of South Hill that looks over the bay.

'The tides in', Robyn observes as they walk together.

Once there Robyn starts to feel very ill. Delilah insists he rests on a rock close to the cliff edge while she goes back to the Cliff Railway station to seek medical assistance.

Robyn starts to panic as his blurred vision is getting increasingly worse. He just about makes out a young man approaching from the town side up the coastal path carrying what looks like a large light blue kite which is almost lost in camouflage against the same blue-toned sky.

'Hello?' he cries with obvious distress in his voice.

The same greeting comes back as the kite carrier gets closer. Robyn's eyes narrow as he seems to recognize the heavy accent.

'Are you experiencing difficulties sir?'

Robyn realizes the voice belongs to the waiter who served them earlier.

'Yes, please get help'. Robyn stands and clutches hold of the kite carrier as he reaches him, who in turn steadies the deteriorating man and repositions him with his back to the sea. Another figure approaches from the opposite end of the path, this time a well-built runner accompanied by a small dog. As he gets closer the runner is seen to be wearing a small rucksack on his back with a tripod sticking up from it. The kite carrier suddenly flicks the kite towards the sky, its extra-large wings springing into life and obscuring any view left for Robyn and any view from the town of anything in front of it. At the same time the runner reaches them and, between gasps of breath, says.

'There you go Robyn; your neighbours will thank me for this.' He wraps the dog lead around Robyn's wrist three or four times as the dog greets his master by jumping up his leg.

'Russell? Is that you?'

'It was.' Replies the runner as he gives Robyn a massively powerful shove which takes his weakened body, along with that of Russell's off the cliff edge and three-hundred and eighteen feet to the rocks below.

The kite is quickly folded cleverly into a miniature version of itself and the kite carrier, accompanied by the runner, leave together towards the Cliff Railway station where they descend the hill on-board the next carriage alongside Delilah.

Victor, Omar and Delilah enter the Michael's Town Market Hall together through the arched entrance and proceed to walk along the large aisle until they reach their individual stalls.

Delilah unlocks her doors with a key, Omar does the same with his a few seconds later via a digital keypad and quickly disappears inside. The Herbalist, Othello, from the stall next to Delilah's steps out into the aisle and asks her how it went. His very thin physique extenuated by a flowery and very tight polyester shirt with bell bottom sleeves.

'The tonic was spot on Othello - good job. You'll have to give me the recipe.' Delilah answers his question cheerfully.

'No chance darling, that one's all mine.'
Victor walks silently straight to his picture framing workshop at the back of the hall. He talks to the occupant of the stall next to his as he begins opening his many locks on the double doors.

'Kite worked a treat.' He said without looking at Odette. A woman in her sixty's replied also without looking away from her unpicking of stitches from what looked like the hem of a pair of trousers.

'So it should. I don't supply shit goods Victor.'

V.O.O.D.O.O.

I

BEGINING OF BLOG: 00:36
Friday, 3 November 2020 (GMT)

I've decided to right this blog, the truth will die with me otherwise and that wouldn't be right. Choose to believe it or not, that's up to you. But I've been sitting on so many secrets and lies over the years I don't know which position I'm happy with anymore. I shuffle a lot. Good or bad, right or wrong, who knows? Never used to give a shit, maybe this blog will help me pull focus on the blurred lines - that is - if I have the time. If this blog suddenly stops or comes to an inclusive abrupt end it means I've been done in - knocked off - assassinated. Most probably by someone who you would never think capable.

My real name is Kian Marc Wilson - haven't written that down for a long time - you won't need to remember it, it's irrelevant and extinct. I'm now known as Victor. A mild mannered, self-employed, forty-four-year-old picture framer. Also, a government backed trained killer.

I know - it sounds like the beginning of a cartoon series from the 1980's - but it's all true. For the first time in my life I'm about to tell the whole truth and nothing but. I work from my workshop at the town's Market Hall alongside five other sole traders who, very successfully, have managed to remain anonymous and keep above suspicion for long before my time - which is now approaching twenty years or so. I was a soldier before that, four-two commando Royal Marines and a stint in the S.B.S. Over the years the people and professions at the Hall have changed but the pseudonyms' have remained the same since the end of world war two.

Othello is the Herbalist. Crystals, candles, and his own home-made remedies. He's a gay Indian who's older than he looks and dresses up every day like a throw-back from the sixties. He is also an expert in poisons and tactical drugs.

Odette is the Quartermaster, as close to a boss as any of us have. She's getting on a bit these days but is still as sharp as one of the pins she uses daily in her seamstress roll at the Hall. Any info is carried though her first. She then delegates one, or several of us to undergo a specific mission and supplies us with whatever equipment we need. She's also in charge of allocating the mission bonuses.

Delilah is the resident florist. She is a beauty who seems to improve with time, and of course knows it. Her role within voodoo is a bit tricky to determine. Seductress? Manipulator might be a better term; she does manage to achieve whatever is needed every time. Ask no questions I suppose.

Omar is a young cheeky, mischievous Arab. His forte is technology, computers and phones mostly. He's the only one that sticks to his specialty both at the Market Hall and within voodoo.

Orien bakes and is often toasted from smoking dope. He's the youngest and most recently recruited member. He's a devout vegan and an explosives and incendiary expert.

Then there's me, Victor the picture framer. Mid-forties and rapidly balding, but still fit enough to carry out my roles of assassination and sabotage. Put my name at the top of the list and we spell out V.O.O.D.O.O.

All six members generally get on well enough. Many have come and gone - voluntarily or not - over the years, but we all maintain a polite and professional working relationship. Odette frowns upon romantic pairings but doesn't mind the occasional social piss up. Othello and Delilah are always going out for drinks together. Something I've noticed over the years is that they're all damaged in some way these days. Each with their own seemingly private and unsociable problem. I remember we all used to open by half seven - there was more fresh goods and flowers back then - only me and Odette left from those days. When the summers were longer and the winters colder. The average opening time is ten now - till around three for most. But of course, none of us need the work. We are paid handsomely - certainly better than any wage packet I ever got from the service I can tell you - with large bonuses for our moonlighting activities thrown in.

But something has happened inside my head recently, like some sort of switch has turned on ... Or maybe off. I can't work it out and need to stop trying. I keep thinking about some of the people I've lost. Girlfriends, colleagues, people I've admired ... All gone ... All dead ... Killed by me. The word in my head was murdered but I wrote killed, as at the time their demises were an inevitable outcome ... There was no choice in the matter. Still isn't now ... not if my plans are endangered. It was all so simple before, black and white but now it's become complicated, with as many greys as a good photocopy.

Ireland was my first - I was nineteen - we called it Halloween. It wasn't the end of October or was there an option of a treat. The tricks were carried out by four of us - the first pair waiting around the back while the second pair knocked the door of the family house.

We had a list. Any male over the height of five-two or wide enough to be a threat were taken down - three silent shots to the torso or one to the head courtesy of a 9mm Browning Hi-power pistol with attached suppressor - you got to know when a single shot was a killer. Unlike the movies, the whole body instantly goes limp before you see the smoke from the gun chamber appear. I proved very good at it and was quickly promoted, eventually commanding men ten years my senior.

It all started to change for me back in December last year.

II

The six members of voodoo didn't make a habit of socializing together, but it was Christmas and Odette had been insistent. So, our pub of choice, and the most remote, was the Crow's Nest situated on the way out of town. It was an odd place - like going back in time once inside. After a few drinks, I got talking to the landlord - I was going on about having to take medication these days to enable me to fly in comfort. The essential mode of transport for my moonlighting activities had slowly become a source of irrational anxiety over the last couple of years. The landlord, an old Navy boy by my reckoning, suggested I stroke a three-foot high sculpture of a crow perched on top of a nondescript pile of rubble, standing proud at the end of the long bar. Very nicely made as it happens. He told me his brother had sculpted it years ago.

'If you want life to travel as the crow flies - you have to caress the crow' he said louder than he'd been talking so far. This proved to be a prompt as a small group of locals, obviously on their Christmas do, sat in the corner with soppy bloody hats on - had started chanting.

'Caress the crow, caress the crow ...'
Thing is I probably would've given it a stroke on my way back to the voodoo lot but that was now out of the question as the chanting had become louder and the whole pub was focused on me. So, I walked past it without a touch and joined my colleagues again under an audible blanket of groans and a couple of boos, which quickly died down once I gave the Christmas party goers a look.

'They say it's come from a research lab, just a few miles away from the epicentre,' Delilah was insistently leaning towards Odette, who as usual was cool as a cucumber.

'When you say they ...'

'The politicians Odette.' Delilah whispers the next bit, 'our bosses.'

'Oh, them. I assume that you are aware that they will say one thing on T.V. and do something completely different in real life, aren't you Delilah?'

'Yes ... But they're talking about stopping flights into the UK from China if the cases rise any further.' Delilah turns here attention towards me, prompting the others to do the same. Something was brewing.

'Victor, you've just come back from that district, did you experience any restrictions?'
I looked at Odette for silent permission to respond, then narrowed my eyes into a scowl.

'That question seems to constitute a massive breach of protocol and confidentiality Delilah. As you know my trip was a solo one and, on a need to know basis.'

'Yes, yes, we all know that Victor, but you were right there weren't you? What, three, four weeks ago. At ground zero?' Delilah's claim was backed up by subtle nods from the rest of the crew.
I was fully aware of the relevance. The job was very simple and very cliché. An attaché case to be delivered to a textile's factory on the outskirts of Wuhan City, China. In and out, no problem. We always knew when the United States was involved in a job because the bonus pay would accelerate significantly. My guess was, not that I paid much attention to it – but on a long hall flight it can't be helped when the case is on your lap the whole time – that it was probably a prototype weapon or some other tech, ready for manufacture or sale. Now however I started to wonder. The coincidence was in favour of the prosecution, who by now were showing more conscience that their professions normally allowed. So, I bit back.

'Why the sudden judgemental attitude? You have all carried out tasks with extreme prejudice before and with no questions asked – so what's with the sudden questioning now?'

'We're not putting any blame on you Victor,' Delilah seemingly speaking for the group again, 'We are just concerned that the organization might have had a hand in this thing, and if so – why?'

63.

'And that's where this conversation ends.' Odette times her forceful statement perfectly as to not have to compete with any other speaker. 'I suggest we all drink up and bugger off home. This seasonal celebration is over - the compliments of the season to you all.'

We had all left the pub in under a minute.

I spent the rest of the evening polishing off the best part of a bottle of scotch whilst catching up on the events surrounding the virus. I'm not one for news most of the time but when it's relevant I make sure the coverage is cross referenced. The British Broadcasting Corporation verses Russia Today is the best example of this. Conflicting biased on the same story enables me to form my own - between the lines - version of events. All the reports seem to suggest that this virus is much more prevalent and deadlier than the SARRS versions we've seen in last few years. The Americans are blaming the Chinese and the Russians are blaming the Americans. The voodoo crew were probably correct. My mundane mission could well have had something to do with the start of this thing. Did I play a part in the introduction of this deadly virus? How bad could it get? It will inevitably reach Europe, but how many will it infect? And what the hell could I do about it?

III

    Christmas came and went in the usual fashion, except for one element. I poached a whole Salmon, twice - once from the river and once again in the oven - and gave what was left to Billy. He's a neighbour from the floor below and well known around Michael's Town. I would often watch him from the flat window. His tatty, thin form going about the business of rummaging in and out of the rubbish bins on the promenade. I envied Billy in a way. A learned man by all accounts, an ex-bank manager, now a one-man recycling unit. He picks up anything he finds discarded on the street or balanced on top, or just inside, the public bins and finds a use for them. He's constantly giving bits and pieces away to local residents or businesses that might make use of them. Hoarding the rest of - god knows what - in his flat, or as I've seen for myself, eating what others won't. I imagine his immune system must be pretty strong by now.

The new year brought with it a tense atmosphere once we all returned to the Market Hall. Small clusters of voodoo members would talk amongst themselves quietly, out of my earshot and keeping an eye out in case I stumbled upon their conversation whilst stepping outside for a cigarette. The social isolation was not a problem, I mostly kept to myself anyway - never been one for chit-chat - but what I found hard to understand was the complete lack of common sense.

These people had some of the strongest minds I'd ever known and yet they seemed to be reacting to every increase in virus cases with uncharacteristic irrational-ism. So, by the time March was close to an end and a national lock-down was announced, I was more than happy to see the Market Hall closed for the duration.

APRIL

The people of Michael's Town, and I suspect the whole island of Cloverdragon, stayed at home - while the sun came out.
Othello, the Herbalist from the Market Hall and voodoo's resident expert in poisons and drugs, had been bugging me for days to meet up with him - outside of course - for a couple of drinks. 'We'll form a bubble' he had said repeatedly. Othello was a flamboyant social addict, so I could understand his obvious desperation for company. I'm sure he had tried to lure in others before me, but we had drunk together on occasion before, and despite our polar opposite personalities, had got on well. He wanted me to go to his place, but it was a ten-mile drive and I flatly refused to stay over. His neighbours would undoubtedly talk. So, weather permitting - and it was - we met at the Marina where we sat on the wall close to the bridge, drinking, smoking and talking - mostly him talking - like a couple of teenagers until dark. Othello told me, amongst other things that really didn't interest me, that some members of voodoo had been kept very busy since the lock-down had been enforced.

'How do you know all this Othello?'

'The group chat of course.' He answered with an obvious tone. 'Haven't you been checking it out?'
I motioned negatively as he threw another question my way.

'How would you know if you got a job, or if Odette wanted intel from you?' He adopted a look of concern.

'She's got my number Othello. It worked just fine before all this book of face shit.' I was playing it cool. In fact, I had taken a glimpse or two of the heavily coded social media site - which took the pretext of a Market Hall Traders Collective - but as my name had not been mentioned I showed no interest.

'You're a proper cowboy, aren't you Victor.

You'd look great inside a 10-gallon hat too, that two-day growth of stubble you've always got, that scar on your chin, and those guns strapped either side of your hips ...'
I had to stop him.
    'It still doesn't explain how you know so much detail Othello.' It worked.
    'Well, it's just like some chemical or homoeopathic compounds really ...'
My eyebrows shot up; I was already lost.
    'Sometimes one and two will equal three Victor. I read between the lines and formulate the most plausible outcome, it's simple.'
    'So, anything in the pipeline for me?' I asked, not expecting the reply I got.
    'Yes. I'm pretty sure that Orien is putting together one of his little toys for a sabotage job - U.S. funded - nice pay-check - sounds like something you'll get to play with soon, don't you think? Due to all the lock-down stuff,' he waved his free hand around his head as if to dismiss it, 'U.S. oil prices have dipped into the negative, it's a record low, so they've got a massive oversupply of crude oil and nowhere to store it.'

The sun had gone, and the tide was in, we suddenly realized we had become cut off from the steps we'd used to get there hours before. Some memorable hilarity ensued as Othello moaned loudly and drunkenly about his ruined shoes and trousers, as we had to dredge ourselves through thigh-high water in order to find dry land.

MAY

It was VE Day, or Victory in Europe Day. Othello had come to my place this time. We sat at the front of the building, behind the railings that divided us from the promenade, and which had just enough room for two chairs and a fold-able table that I had carried down from the flat above. We lined up the drinks, Othello turned up his sleeves and trouser bottoms and sat back enjoying the hot sun which relentlessly beamed down on us from a cloudless blue sky. It was early, just before eleven, but as I opened the first of many cans of beer I thought and said, 'what the hell.'

As the morning seamlessly became early afternoon, the population on the prom had grown from the usual dog and power walkers to lots of clusters of people. Some pretending to accidentally meet whilst on their permitted hour of exercise. They would talk for a while and then look nervously around before cautiously sitting together - as one big group - on the beach. The so-called innocent meeting scenario blown out of the water once a couple from the group started producing disposable barbecues and bottles of booze from small rucksacks and plastic bags. One of these groups included Orien the Baker-come explosives and incendiary devises expert, from the Market Hall. He had spent ten years in bomb-disposal and was the newest and youngest member of voodoo, that's all I knew. I nudged Othello, who either had his eyes closed or couldn't see a damn thing through those very big and very dark sunglasses of his.

'Orien.' I said flatly and pointed towards the horizon.

'Where?' He had to remove the Elton John's to see accurately. 'Oh yah. He's with his stoner-mates.' He added disapprovingly.

'Yah, he's really into his ganja, right? It's not just the way he is?' I had often wondered. I'd known a couple of local guys in Iraq for a while. They were paid to supply safe houses, show us back alley routes and gather intel from the street. They were real cool customers and had no translatable word for anxiety. Later I'd discovered that they would knock themselves out with opium every night, the effects of which were obviously still in their systems for the duration of the next day. It explained why they could only work with us until sixteen-hundred-hours. But I thought maybe Orien was born with nerves of steel which helped him to excel in his line of work.

'Yes, he's a massive pot-head.' Othello answered my question with brutish accuracy. 'Hay! Orien. Choo wee!'

Orien came over followed by some of his friends but stayed on the prom side of the railings.

'Hay gents, partaking in a little partying our we?' Orien's smile showed his dark-line-stained teeth. Othello and Orien exchanged pleasantries with Othello wanting to know exactly what Orien's plans were for the rest of the day.

'We're off to Jacqui's Town in a bit. Going to the Uni to protest with the Chinese students.' Orien gave a limp clenched-fisted pump to the air.

'Is that wise?' I asked. 'In your position I mean, getting involved with a political movement?'

'What you gotta understand man ...' Orien's flippant attitude instantly annoyed me. 'Is that China is about to vote for a Hong Kong security legislation, which is aimed at preventing external interference in affairs in Hong Kong, criminalize any act that threatens national security and also allow the State Council to set up a national security agency in Hong Kong when needed. There's thousands already organizing protests out there.' He lent over the railings and beckoned us towards him as he whispered. 'This is Chinas reaction to the germ-warfare virus claim being introduced on their soil and that's how they'll get rid of western intelligence sources currently based in Hong Kong. Yah? Got it?'

'Got it!' Othello answered, uninterested as he sat back in his chair and put his sunglasses back on. 'Well you kids have fun.'

'Yah man, fun.' Orien produced a long, creased and slightly bent joint from his pocket and prepared to light it. I'd been looking over his shoulder as he spoke, at two police officers, one of each sex.
The little bits of blue told me that they were only specials and had no real power to do much at all, but I could without the attention.

'Hay Orien, do me a favour and take it onto the beach? And watch yourself over there, huh!' I gestured towards the part-time police couple coming up parallel to us across the road.

'Oh, yah. Ok well you crazy cats have a good one and I'll see you when we all get back to the hum-drum.'

Orien through us a two-fingered salute that I could have taken as an insult, my grandfather would of recognized as a sign of victory, and my son - if I had one - would no doubt of taken as Orien had intended, whatever the hell that was.

'Is it three o'clock yet?' I asked Othello who was lounging so had missed the salute.

'Not far off probably.' He didn't bother to check his watch. 'Why?'

'I've got a bottle of Gin upstairs, won it in a raffle. What'd think?'

'Crack it open you crazy cat.' Othello's smirk was infectious.

Later the sound of Vera Lynn came out - slightly distorting at the crescendos - from one of the buildings on the terrace. We quickly discovered it was the air force blue B&B two doors down. Presumably the owner was ex-air force as he had erected two angled flag holders to the front of the old Georgian styled house, one housed a large Union Jack and the other, the Royal Air Force insignia. The old tunes prompted questions from Othello about my service days, the details of which I've always kept out of my head, together with any compulsion to let out of my mouth, but as usual he pressed me for answers.

'Kosovo, Ireland, Sierra Leone, South America, Afghanistan and Iraq.' That's all he got. 'And you Othello, I'm guessing M.I.5. straight out of University?'

'Indian Army actually, well military intelligence mostly. I had to get out though. My - urm - lifestyle? Had got me into some trouble and subsequently banished from the family home. Luckily someone kind in the department recommended me for - you were nearly right about that - Vauxhall Cross, London.'

'M.I.6 …' I only half said. I'd spotted Delilah - it was hard not too - walking in our direction with her young daughter from some distance away.

'S.I.S., it's now called Victor. The Secret Intelligence Service.' Othello noticed I wasn't paying him any attention. 'Although it's all a bit of a bloody joke.

When I started, I would travel to work by bus, and one particular driver would announce 'all spy's off!' at my stop. Would you believe it? Victor!'
I apologized and told him Delilah was heading our way.

We exchanged pleasantries while Delilah told her daughter to carry on until she reached the railings at the end of the prom and warned her not to descend the steps that led to the Marina beyond it.

'Give me a voodoo mission over this bloody home-schooling any day of the week. Is that Gin?' Delilah didn't wait for confirmation, just grabbed the bottle with her perfectly manicured, slender hand and took a large, un-lady-like, gulp. 'It's bloody torturous! - Oh darling, I told you no!' She moved off to retrieve the girl from the Marina steps while elegantly twisting her neck around towards us.

'I'll have another one of those on the way back boys!' Even her shout was somehow, smooth, and her hair blew in a wind that wasn't there.

'I'll get you a glass!' I shouted back.

'Don't bother!' Delilah replied, quieter this time and with a less grace.

'You two got a thing going on Victor?' Othello asked, predictably. I had noticed over the last few weeks that he was compelled to make comment on anybody within our line of sight.

'Delilah? No Othello, nothing to gossip about there I'm afraid.'

'She told me that you had a little thing.' Othello was teasingly sheepish.

'What the hell does that mean?' I was too aggressive for Othello, who sat up defensively.

'You two had a little fling, that's all I meant Victor.'

'OK.' I felt the need to put him at ease. Despite this, he quickly changed the subject.

'I have a son you know, back in India. My parents hold joint custody along with his mother. They have successfully replaced their first son - disgraced - with the grandson. He has just become a junior officer in the Indian Army.'

'Pass me your glass Othello, lets fill em' up before Delilah comes back.' He did - and she did, taking the rest of the bottle I offered her. 'Land of Hope and Glory' bled out of the air force blue B&B as people started to leave the beach for home.

JUNE

I had succumbed to Othello's incessant nagging and agreed to spend the evening at his place. He picked me up in his car, with intention that I would catch the late train home that night, it had just started running again.
Freeman's Bay is a small, quiet village about ten miles north of Michael's Town and famous for its annual Mardi-Gras celebrations - cancelled this year of course. Othello's place was as I had expected, and then some. Very white, clean and devoid of any clutter. The whole place looked like a new Hotel room complete with complimentary coffee and tea making facilities, even having dried flowers and orchids on most surfaces. I was ushered through the one-story house and outside into the garden. It met the sandy beach of Freeman's Bay and instantly felt like a world away from Michael's Town in its gloriousness. Othello had already prepared the first drinks of the day. A green liquid and fruit filled, tall, beautifully crafted blown glass jug with two glasses to match, perched on an equally elegant table, which is where we sat.

'It's a Green Demon cocktail Victor and tastes like honeydew and lemon. It's all about the melon flavour of the Midori cut with the tartness of lemon juice.' Othello poured the drinks as he spoke. 'You'll also find some vodka and rum in it. Just in case you were thinking it might not have enough kick for you.'

'Thank you.' I struggled a bit with the thinness of the glass and the largeness of the fruit.

'Makes my plastic tumblers and cheap Gin look positively common Othello.' I was being deliberately disingenuous.

Othello went on to tell me all about Omar - the Mobile Phone and Computer repair man at the Market Hall, come I.T. expert for voodoo. Over the last week, Omar had apparently lost the ability to track and research individual's private data due to a massive lawsuit involving a famous search engine site, which had spun-out the normally happy-go-lucky, cheeky-chappy - Othello's words not mine. The second jug of Green Demon came out, he was right it did have a decent kick although very easy to drink.

'So, I thought in light of recent events it might be nice to ask Omar round. We could have a little three-some.' Othello didn't mean it in the way I'd initially taken it, but it made me uncomfortable, nevertheless.

'No can do.' I announced unforgivably.

'What!' Omar clutched his chest with emotional discomfort.

'I've got a job on, abroad.' I explained.

'Oooh ... hadn't heard about that one, do tell Victor.'

'Why?' I was being rightfully clandestine.

'Now come on Victor. I've told you loads of juicy goss.' Othello started to wriggle in his seat so much I had to raise my hand in submission as I drank.

'Alright Othello, you'll probably find out anyway, you seem to have a knack for that, you should be in intelligence. I'm off to Siberia.'

'Ouch ... Cold. What for?' Othello was engrossed, so I whispered to exaggerate his eagerness.

'First I've got to pick up a little toy from Orien before I leave. I'm to stick it to a fuel tank at a power plant near Norilsk.'

'Kaboom! I told you, didn't I Victor? Othello filled a paused moment. I nodded and hummed twice in acknowledgment and wondered if I should elaborate or not. His wide-eyed enthusiasm and my somewhat stewed state inspired me to do so.

'Over twenty-thousand tons of oil will spill into the Ambarnaya River once the fuel tank collapses.

Putin will have to declare a state of emergency and the good old U.S. of A will suddenly have a market and a place to store their surplus oil stocks.'

'Shit Victor, your stuff is proper macho - in it?'

'It's what I do Othello.' I said coolly as I took another drink and raised an eyebrow. Othello found the over-acting hilarious. His laugh, together with the green booze was infectious enough to set me off as well.

Othello's mobile phone pulsed, and his expression was one of genuine surprise. Despite Othello's outward confidence, I don't think he had anybody to call a friend. Why else would I be here otherwise? Over the top of my glass I saw his eyes widened even further as he read the caller I.D. and answered instantly. Othello's Indian dialect was more like high pitched ranting from the offset, it calmed a bit later but then finished with a definitive insult. Othello didn't look at me just buried his face in his hands and wept. I did nothing for a while, then poured the last of the Green Demon into one glass.

It was intended for me, but I found myself touching Othello's arm with the glass and miming a cheers motion once his pink eyes appeared from behind his dampened hands. I thought the thin black lines surrounding his eyes were a natural feature but now they were smudged, with the odd line running a dark-grey skid-mark down his almost skeletal cheek line. Even in his obviously distressed state, Othello could not stop himself from talking for more than a couple of minutes at a time.

'That was my mother - in India. It's my son Victor, the officer in the Indian Army?'
I showed him I had remembered with a nodding head.

'He's been killed - along with twenty other soldiers in a clash with Chinese forces at the Kashmir Region - disputed Himalayan boarder area.'

'I'm sorry Othello. I've heard it is a terrible thing to lose a child.' It was completely insincere, but the best I could do. I just didn't feel anything. 'Let's hope the shot was an accurate one and death was as quick as it undoubtedly was dignified.'

'There was no exchange of fire Victor.' Othello

continued to sob whilst I mentally searched for a possible way in which a clash that did not involve an exchange of fire could prove so lethal.

'My mother told me that he was beaten to death with rocks and clubs.'

I needed to get back. The summer hedonism, as it was - was over.

IV

JULY

Once the Market Hall re-opened for business, we were all surprisingly busy, both with customers and voodoo obligations. Delilah told me I looked good. My skin was coffee-coloured and my hair, what little of it there was left, had lighted considerably.

AUGUST

My summer tan turned to sunburn on a trip to Beirut. The mandate was simple enough. I was to collect an R.P.G. Rocket-propelled grenade - from a local source and break up a secret meeting taking place at the port. The code used was cleaning house.
The warhead sparked a detonation of ammonium nitrate housed in a tank immediately behind the eight subjects. The blast was the biggest I've ever seen or felt. Despite my long-range position, I got burnt, my shirt blown clean off my back, and I spent the duration of the flight back to the UK mainland in perpetual semi-blindness.

Odette was spending a lot of time in America, something to do with the up and coming election for president, Othello had told me, but for once had very little more to add.
Orien had returned from briefly joining Odette as news of deadly wildfires erupted from California to Washington state, burning millions of acres and displacing hundreds of thousands of people. I'd started watching the news again, big mistake.

SEPTEMBER

I hadn't been back to the Market Hall since catching the news of a massive explosion at the Beirut port, sparked by the accidental detonation of 2,750 tons of ammonium nitrate. It killed at least 190 people and injured thousands of others. I felt nauseous all the time. I needed a distraction, a sense of normality - shit - I needed a miracle.
I heard the Crow's Nest Pub was closing down, probably for good, and the brewery were selling off some of the fixtures. I got in touch and reserved the crow sculpture. I'm sure it's the only thing I've ever bought for myself that isn't purely functional. I own no pictures, ironically have no frames on the walls, no trinkets, no mementos. Nothing that tells my story. It's all been unconsciously designed to be left behind - as it is - at a moment's notice. Not so much Feng Shui - more Fuck It.
Using the van, I picked up the crow sculpture from the almost lifeless pub, which smelt faintly of death, and gave it the rub I should have last Christmas on the way out.

Once I got back to the promenade, I couldn't park anywhere near the flat, the Motor-homes had landed. Some of them looked very impressive. Not the familiar sun-stained white plastic versions with light blue wave motifs running down the side, but black and grey shark-like long-wagons with smooth edge-less lines. I wondered what retirement might be like living in one. Another first. Isolation out in the open - anywhere you like. The sculpture was heavy, so I stopped at a bench on the promenade halfway to the flat. It was quiet, just as quiet as it had been in lock-down. The usual gulls seemed to be outnumbered by scores of crows.
I watched them, two of which were having a standoff, lifting their wings and spreading feathers to make themselves look bigger. They fought, pecking and butting each other, one trying to get the other on to its back. They weren't even fighting over food, there seemed to be no reason for the violence.

Some of the other birds looked on while the seniors just went about their normal business. One got the upper hand and pinned down the weaker, it kept on spearing the floored crow until I could see blood on its beak. I was transfixed on the weaker, now injured, bird on the ground until the clapping of my hands brought me back and sent off all the crows at the same moment. I stood over the injured crow lying on its back with only the ability to move one wing with an intermittent twitch. Its tongue vibrated as it screamed loudly in pain and fear. I looked at the sculpture standing on the bench behind me. I'm not superstitious in any way but, I should have given it a rub back at Christmas - felt like years ago now. 'Things might have stayed sane if I had.' I thought as I placed one foot on the body of the bird and extinguished any remaining life out of it using a short, sharp kick to the head with the other. The crow was still.

In some sort of exhausted sleep but the scene between my feet was an ultra-violent one. The sight was one of untidy rest, with an absence of any sense of peace. And there it was ... That's when I felt it. It was like I'd just swallowed half an apple without chewing and my throat had closed up after it had passed - in a sort of demonstration of discomfort. My eyes felt like they were burning, only to be cooled by a small eruption of liquid. I had to look away from the dead crow. This was new ... and I didn't like it. It was just a bird for Christ sake.

Once I got into the flat, I found a place for the heavy sculpture and found myself talking to it.
    'They're you go, looking good.' I placed my hand on the bird at the very top and let my fingers genially explore every contour as I slowly worked my way downwards to the base, then repeated the process.
    'Caress the crow - they'd said - to make life straight forward - as the crow flies.' At that moment, I wished I was a crow.

V

OCTOBER

The end of October brought with it a chill in the air and new lock-down restrictions. This time they called it a Fire-break; it would end after the first week of November. The Market Hall was again to close. We had to stay in touch with Odette of course via the private social media group or, in the case of particularly sensitive information sharing, a physical meeting would be arranged in the form of a walk along Elm Tree Avenue, which is where I met her on a not-too-cold gloriously sunny afternoon in the late days of the month.

'I'd like you to have one of your little chats with this man.' Odette handed me a tennis ball which was far too large a toy for her ridiculously hairy Pekingese who was gliding leglessly a couple of meters in front of us. 'All the intel you need is inside.' Odette had a way of talking covertly that sounded like she was reading a bedtime story to a child, even if the narrative would be deemed inappropriate.
I gently squeezed the ball revealing a neat slit along the seam with the strong autumn sunlight illuminating a white piece of folded paper inside.

'Could prove difficult to travel at the moment,' I pointed out.

'Not a problem. His workplace is local - Percival Medical Science Centre.'

'Handy.' I was genuinely surprised.
The Medical Centre was no more than a mile away. Odette stopped to pick up a Pekingese dropping using her hand inside a small black plastic bag and scanned the locality before resuming.

'This one is vital Victor; it's come from the highest level. His name is Dr. Callahan, he's head pathologist at the Centre and is threatening to go public about the level, or lack of, interest that central government have had concerning the virus rates and the possibility of a vaccine code being proposed from his department.'

'You want the code, right?'

'No, we want him shut up, and if not - shut down.'

'Why?' I realized what I had just said as Odette stop dead in her tracks staring forward. We don't use words like can't, won't, why and on who's orders. 'Sorry, ignore that.' I quickly rectified the mistake, yet another first for me, and Odette strolled on as if someone had just pressed the play button.

'You will report using the group chat via the usual platform, referencing the subject as the large potted plants at the entrance of the Market Hall. The codename for Callahan is Chrysanthemum -
Picked is contact confirmation -
Potted will indicate co-operation has been reached - and Add to the compost will equate as elimination of the threat. It's all in the ball Victor.' Again, Odette had timed her speech perfectly. We had reached the gates of the avenue. Little did I know then, as I watched her carry the Pekingese in her arms across the road and continue along, that the next time we'd meet would be in very different circumstances.

THURSDAY 29 OCT

It was still sunny the next morning, which made my plan to head off Dr. Callahan as he got to his car ready to go to work, an easy option. The warning off became an exchange which proved very interesting and one which would subsequently change my life forever. Callahan was not surprised when I climbed into the passenger seat of his car as he'd tried, and failed to start it, the spark plug safely tucked in my trouser pocket. In fact, he hinted that he had been waiting for some sort of contact. He had balls this guy. And no time to waste.

'Look, tough guy, do what you want. The medical council already have my report on the government's dereliction of duty - but nothing is going to stop me trying to get my vaccine code to my colleges in Brussels. Discredit me, lock me out of my lab, shit break my hands if you have to, just get on with it or fuck off!'

None of the options interested me, what did was the vaccine, or the possibility of a vaccine I should say.

'Will it work?' My question was calmly subdued. He answered in such a formulaic way that it sounded like the hundredth time he'd had to say it.

'It's mostly based on research already carried out for the SARRS vaccine. Dropped at the crucial moment of course because the virus burnt itself out and the authorities didn't want to throw any more money at it. The concept is straight forward enough - it works at a cellular level - introducing a minute version of the virus, in one or possibly two doses, into the system encouraging your natural immune system to adapt in order to fight it. It will need trailing of course but the advantage is that there's plenty of A symptomatic and freshly recovered subjects around to push for human trials very soon after the animal tests. So yes, in my opinion it will work - but it must begin now! If the virus mutates enough times it will eventually find its way around the bloody thing and we won't be able to catch up. I told the government all this last year. To shut down air travel, schools, non-essential workplaces, and ban mass gatherings. Wash your hands, keep distances and wear a mask in public. They ignored me and now the bastards are using my very own words on their hazardous waste style posters. Now if there's nothing else ...?'

'Look, doctor - I'm breaking protocol here but - I want to help.' As I spoke a surge of adrenaline shot up my abdomen from my naval to my throat - it felt like - new life - liberating. Callahan missed it.

'Then fix my bloody car and let me continue the work - I'm at the last stage. I can send my findings to Brussels in two days.' He counted the days by aggressively hitting the steering wheel. I was in professional mode again.

My heart rate back to the lie detector busting, marching band beat it was used to.

'You're in danger Callahan.'

'Where'd the doctor go?' He interrupted cynically.

'I'm talking about real danger. They will stop you - one way or the other - they sent me to do just that.'

'So, if you don't, someone else will, right?' He got it.

'But I only need two days...'

'You won't get them - we move fast.' Callahan looked dejected. Another strain on a man that looked almost strained out. He needed a shave, shower and sleep judging by his appearance and aroma.

'I might have a plan,' I said, 'but you will have to give up all access to your lab by tomorrow.' Callahan nodded.

'And for Christ sake have a shower.'

Victor Clear Cut Picture Framing
regarding the plants outside
the entrance to the market hall -
the chrysanthemum is picked.
Thur 10:31

Odette Stitched Up Alterations
is it potted?
Thur 10:35

Victor Clear Cut Picture Framing
i need a little more time for that.
Thur 10:37

Odette Stitched Up Alterations
there is no more time - it was
made clear to you that if it
could not be potted - you must
add to the compost.
Thur 10:39

Victor Clear Cut Picture Framing
it's not ready for the compost -
it shows great promise.
Thur 10:40

Odette Stitched Up Alterations
promise or not - you must
add to the compost.
Thur 10:41

Victor Clear Cut Picture Framing
i feel strongly that we should
give it a chance - could be
important for the future.
Thur 10:42

Odette Stitched Up Alterations
if you cannot add the
chrysanthemum to the compost
- your position at the market
hall will be in doubt.
Thur 10:45

Victor Clear Cut Picture Framing
i will not dispose of something
that could bring hope back to the
world - sorry.
Thur 10:46

Odette Stitched Up Alterations
i therefore have no alternative
than to inform you that your
membership to the market hall
is suspended with immediate affect
- all privileges and rights that
come with it are hereby cancelled.
Thur 10:50

Odette Stitched Up Alterations
any further contact with the
chrysanthemum is forbidden
- another member will deal with that
- you will be contacted shortly
concerning your future at the
market hall.
Thur 10:52

```
After turning off the phone and putting up a sign that
read Gone Hunting in the window of the workshop at the
closed Market Hall, I walked back to the flat just in
time to catch Billy on his way out, armed with empty
plastic bags ready for the filling of.
```

He asked me how I was. It took me a moment before I told him that I actually felt really good - I mean better than I had for years. I might have played a part in something terrible before Christmas, but now - and for the first time in my life - I might just have the chance to help put it right. No matter what the cost.
Once inside I poured myself a scotch, then promptly threw it away. This one is big Odette had said, comes from the highest level. That's when I realized, I could be in big trouble here.
I knew I had to get Callahan to safety, but the first thing to do was to find out where Odette lived. Get control of her and you've got voodoo by the balls.

VI

FRIDAY 30 OCT

Finding Odette's house proved easy. I knew she lived somewhere in the vicinity of South Hill, the large landmark that dominated the skyline at the southern end of the promenade. I had framed some photographs she had taken from her sitting room, of the big storm back in 2014. Armed with a pair of curtains, I'd taken down from the flat, I soon found a couple walking their dogs. A few innocent questions later, about the seamstress who said she'd fix my curtains at home despite lock-down, soon resulted in the couple literally pointing out the specific location to me. Odette's house was halfway up the hill. It was unique in the fact that it was the only modern looking property in the area, an oddity for Cloverdragon. It had a large square design with mostly glass visible. Cameras everywhere no doubt. I got no closer, that will have to wait.

I dumped the curtains back at the flat and took a drive out to my personal safe-house, the next intended destination for Callahan. It's at the edge of the woods at Clover Sands, close to the most northern point of the east of the island. It's under twenty miles, as the crow flies, but can take up to three hours to get there. The roads through Screaming Mountains National Park have enough bends to challenge even the French National Rally Team.

    The safe-house was as I'd left it, some five years ago - when I was last suspended from voodoo. Omar had called me into his Mobile Phone and Computer Repair Stall at the Market Hall. He looked very serious, a rare event. I remember that it made him look older and meant one of two things.

He had found something out and felt the need to tell me before Odette - or he was lining me up for one of his practical jokes, a dangerous thing to do, as he, and his nose, had previously discovered. As it happened it was the former. His cousin had left a laptop for repair with Omar that very morning. I didn't want to watch the video Omar had found and by the end, wished I hadn't. What got to me the most was the absence of any crying. Five men - if you can call them that - and three very young children. They looked like siblings. The oldest did start to cry at the beginning of the roughly shot video, until a grossly overweight adult ordered another to silence her - in a way I refuse to describe. Omar wouldn't watch it again. Instead he kept watch by the closed door of his stall, constantly telling me to turn down the volume a little. Despite the harrowing scenes witnessed on the laptop, I kept a steady resolve, as I do - as I did - and asked Omar what it had to do with voodoo i.e. - me?

'Take it to the police.' I suggested.

'No, the bloody cops are no good. The guys in the video will just deny it was them. Police think we all look alike anyway. All the abusers have to do is grow or shave a beard or two and become unrecognisable to most juries.

'You know all of them Omar?'

'Yes, charity workers and community leaders most of them.' He said. 'I just want them taught a lesson Victor.
A hard one you know. Make sure they don't even think about doing anything like that again.'
Omar was great at his job and had been on assignments in some of the most dangerous places on earth, but often he would be naive to the western world he now chose to live in.

'Omar, you know that a broken nose or two will heel in time,' I said, 'but this sort of sickness will never be cured, no matter what you do.'
Omar pleaded with me to put a stop to it until I agreed, after all he'd done me enough favours over the last couple of years.

86.

I found three of the abusers in Omar's cousins' kitchen. They put up a surprisingly strong fight, so they had to be put down, for good. Each one getting one of my 'V's' in their own blood, upside down on their foreheads. I only award a 'V' to someone whom truly deserves it. I'm careful not to award enough 'V's' locally for it to be noticed by the inept authorities on Cloverdragon.

It was getting late by the time I arrived back from my safe-house to Michael's Town. I contacted Callahan and told him everything was in place and he could move out of his home tonight. He refused, saying he had some last-minute tests to verify concerning the vaccine theory and wanted his wife's safety prioritized over his. We discussed the situation for a while with Callahan suggesting places where his wife might be safe. I chose the best option. Telling him that she must be collected, not to take the car herself or use public transport, and she must leave by the morning at the latest.

I went on to instruct Callahan that I will escort him to the lab first thing. From then on, he will stay with me until I can get him to my safe-house at Clover Sands.

They'll be no turning back then. Voodoo will come after us. It'll be me verses them - an awesomely formidable foe.

END OF PART I

ALL THIS TIME

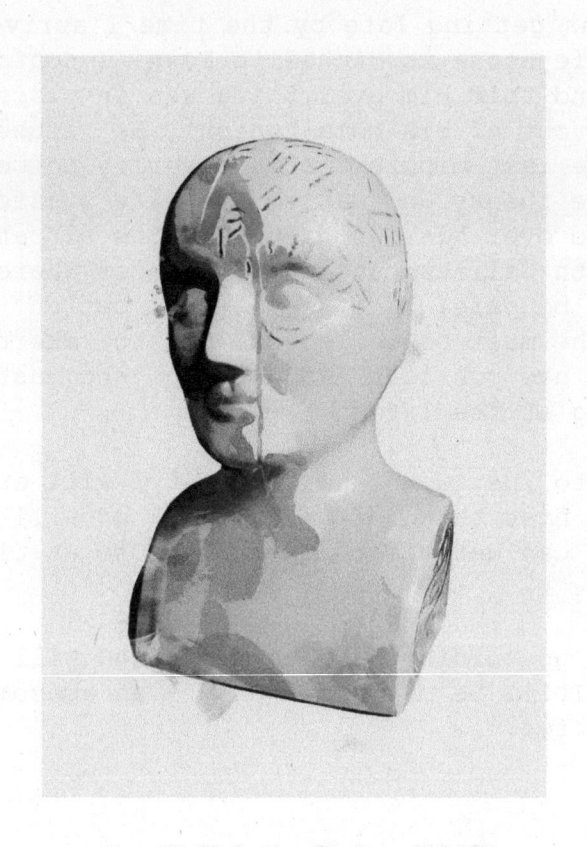

COPYCAT

COPYCAT

CHAPTER 1
(MAY 2020)

Audience applaud politely.

A couple in their mid-forties are traveling though the Cloverdragon countryside in a car.

NEIL: I'm telling you - once the holidaymakers pour in from over the border, in the next month or so - the numbers will rise.

DOT: I'm glad you're speaking to me now. The thought of spending the next month or two at the cabin, without you even talking was - well - pointless.

NEIL: Then you've got the students of course - in September - thousands of them from all over the country and beyond. - I would hope they'll stop the international ones.

DOT: Do you think a couple of months is enough? - Neil.

NEIL: What?

DOT: Do you think two months isolated at my dad's cabin will be long enough for this thing to fizzle out?

A distant cough from an audience member.

Neil stays silent for a time that is uncomfortable.

NEIL: Callahan reckons it's been around since before Christmas. Most of the cases coming into the lab were very old and had classic symptoms of pneumonia, so nothing unusual for the time of year - until of course - January.

DOT: When China hit the news, right?

NEIL: It was already here. It's got very little to do with China. Callahan's theory is that it all stems back to de-forestation ...

DOT: The bats you mean ...

NEIL: No - not bloody bats - well not directly anyway, Callahan says the de-forestation aids the extinction of the larger mammals - so in turn the smaller ones thrive.

DOT: Like bats.

NEIL: More likely, the rodents.

DOT: Rats? Like the plague!

Muted laughter from the audience.

NEIL: Callahan thinks he's discovered two strains already. The condition of some of the organs I took samples from were - shocking - complete deterioration leading to inevitable shut down. They hardly needed a Histology report to ascertain that.

DOT: My god! - Didn't you say that Doctor Callahan had reported it ages ago?

NEIL: He submitted a report to Wilson, whom dragged his feet, with the insistence that he pass it onto Blair, head of department, who did report the findings to the national council. Weeks past with Callahan putting the pressure on Wilson, until a message from the home office eventually got delivered down the line. Blah, blah, will take into consideration, blah, blah, findings remain confidential, blah, blah, forget about it basically. And don't tell anyone.

DOT: That's immoral!

NEIL: Tell me about it. In the last five years we've seen around fifteen similar viruses with the potential that this one has - but not quite as aggressive.

DOT: What?

NEIL: Callahan's report recommended the stopping of flights into the UK - quarantine for the ex-pats returning - using a tag system - and start testing, tracking and tracing straight away - and even mentioned the symptoms, along with a new cough and high temp, of the loss of taste and smell, it's called anosmia - and the need to wear protective masks in public. Otherwise autumn and winter will be disastrous, this is called seasonality.

DOT: And they ignored the report?

NEIL: Basically, told him to shut up.

DOT: How was he, when you asked for extended leave?

NEIL: I didn't ask him, I told him.

DOT: So, we're getting out - to the cabin - twenty miles from the nearest building ...

NEIL: Twenty-one.

Another uncomfortable silence.

DOT: Look Neil, about last night ...

NEIL: I don't want to discuss it.

DOT: Well that much is obvious - but I do think we'll have to at some point. You should've had that drink last night - might have loosened you up a bit.

NEIL: Oh well yes - of course - that's what I should've done - got pissed and ranted about you having an affair - which is probably my fault in the first place for not providing you with children.

DOT: I told you last night. It's over - and it had nothing to do with you or the fact that we never had kids.

NEIL: Hate that word!

DOT: I know. I said I'd prove it to you - so look!

The car comes to a swift halt - but without skidding.

NEIL: What the hell? Why did you throw your phone out of the window? We'll never find that now.

DOT: That's the idea Neil, start anew.

NEIL: I'm not travelling sixty odd miles back to town to get you a new one!

DOT: Fine - like I said - start-a-new, but this time, just us, alone in the cabin.

NEIL: Make or break you mean.

DOT: I suppose so - yes. - It's certainly a test of any relationship - if we can avoid the 'fever', well, there lies the hope.

NEIL: Well the weather's due to be good, so we shouldn't be cooped up indoors for too long with those creaking walls.

DOT: I always thought you liked the refurbishment. You and dad were always talking about the improvements he had made since our last visit.

NEIL: Yes, there was always a new armchair or table or something, must be pretty cluttered there by now.

DOT: Dad always used to pick up stuff at the Flea Market, often brought back the fleas with it too. He was trying to recreate something I think, either from a description in a book or a childhood memory of some kind, I think.

NEIL: Something from one of his own novels maybe?

DOT: No, far too traditional. The novels were always set in the city. I remember when we were kids - sorry - children, he spent hours caving out the panels and making the cupboards for the walls, it was more spacious before those went up, floor to ceiling of course, I'm sure he was modelling the decor on an old horse drawn caravan - a showman's home or something you know? It was like everything could be locked away or secured down, ready for transit.

NEIL: Wonder how he got the cabin onto those stilts?

DOT: He got in a crane; same time he had the bathroom delivered - that was a relief for all of us I can tell you.

NEIL: Yes, of course the shipping container come plumbed bathroom - ingenious that.

DOT: Before that arrived, we had to go in the trees. Mind you it can still be a bit of a pain in the middle of the night. A fifty-meter mad dash across wet grass always wakes me up more than I'd like.

NEIL: How long would you lot spend there when you were young?

DOT: Dad visited three or four times a year, for weeks on end - to write his great British novel - he hadn't published yet. But we would only visit in the summer, maybe for a week or so.

NEIL: You always said he was a selfish bastard.

DOT: I know - but mum and him used to argue a lot when he was at home, and as I've got older I've started to think that going to the cabin was his way, in a round-about way - of keeping the family together.

NEIL: Didn't work though did it. Your mother eventually buggered off with that Italian. What was he twelve or something?

Muted laughter from the audience.

DOT: Marco was twenty-four when they met, and as you well know was a lovely man. His only fault was that he just drove too bloody fast that's all.

A reflective silence.

NEIL: Well I felt sorry for your father - think I was the only one.

DOT: I never blamed my mum for leaving him - he was obsessed with his bloody books - you've read a few. I mean the main character, Marvin Hawk was a rough, tough, chauvinistic and direct law man, for Christ sake he was everything dad wasn't and everything Marco was.

NEIL: His books, provided a very nice lifestyle for you lot though didn't they, very nice indeed. What was it? Twenty novels, four best sellers, that's a hell of a lot of work, and wonga, whether you like it or not. And I've never heard you or your sisters ever moan about that.

DOT: Mum would've preferred a modest life with some sort of normality, rather than a luxurious, lonely one.

NEIL: So, she chose an out-of-work Italian waiter with a need-for-speed instead. - Like mother - like daughter.

Audience ooooh ...

DOT: You know sometimes, you can be more of a bastard than my dad ever was.

Dot sobs for a moment

NEIL: Dot, I'm sorry. You know I loved your mother. We turn off here do we?

DOT: No, it's the next one – there used to be a sign for the Honey Farm on the turn.

NEIL: Yes, there it is, you can just see what's left of it though the hedge.

DOT: Keep going down, it narrows quite a bit until you think you've reached a dead end - there it is look - the old cattle gate is hidden between the trees on the right - I'll get out and open it.

The car wheel-spins its way through the soft ground into a large clearing surrounded by tall trees. Neil parks in the space between the cabin and converted shipping container come bathroom and joins his wife out of the car.

NEIL: Bloody hell that gate could do with some grease couldn't it?

DOT: What? Oh, it must have been open already when you came last time. It has always been very loud - it's deliberate - acts as a sort of organic early warning come motion detector device.

NEIL: Christ - sounds like a wounded animal. I'll get the bags from the boot, you open up.

DOT: Leave the bags, there's no rush and the car's close enough we can get them anytime.

NEIL: I want the room Dot; I'm going to go to the village for a months' worth of supplies. I explained all this to you last week - in the next few days things will be running out, especially if this lock-down continues any longer. I've got the list right here, remember?

DOT: Yes, of course, sorry I forgot.

Dot walks towards the cabin with Neil shouting after her as he unloads the car.

NEIL: I'll catch you up. We need to check the electric and plumbing. Any problems and I can get someone from the village to sort it before everyone stops working altogether.

DOT: Watch this first step Neil. I think the frost has got to it last winter.

Neil follows Dot into the cabin.

NEIL: Hay there's some lovely stuff in here. Look at those sofa beds. That's my chair right there.

DOT: The water looks clear Neil - look.

NEIL: Nice pint glass too. Where did he get all this stuff, it seems to fit perfectly?

DOT: Dad used to make most of it - these folding chairs tuck under the kitchen table see.

NEIL: Very clever I must say.

DOT: And then the table itself can extend to accommodate oh, six people quite comfortably.

NEIL: Amazing, think of the room we could save at home with some of this stuff.

DOT: Room for what Neil, we've got plenty as it is.

NEIL: How's the electric?

DOT: Kettles on.

NEIL: Oh. How do we pay for it?

DOT: We don't, dad had it wired into the main somehow, same with the plumbing.

NEIL: Tight git! - Bloody hot in here isn't it.

DOT: I'll open some windows and give the cooking pans a once over while you pop to the village.

NEIL: Pop, hah, it's twenty-one bloody miles away to Wolves Hill. I'll check over the bathroom on the way out.

DOT: Okay. Hey Neil - Did you tell Gruff we were bailing out for up to a couple of months?

NEIL: Did I hell!

DOT: Oh Neil, I told Helen, so she could keep an eye on things - they are our neighbours after all.

NEIL: Neighbours, that's a joke. Sod him, why should I tell him anything - when he cuts down that bloody bush that's killing the sunlight into my study - then I'll be civil.

CHAPTER 2
(JUNE 2020)

Dot and Neil are sitting outside on a very hot day.

DOT: I can't believe it's been a week already, since we arrived.

NEIL: I bloody can. A week without T.V. and no bugger around to buy one from. We could have ordered online if you hadn't chucked your sodding phone out of the car window. I must admit though - I thought you'd miss it - your phone I mean. You're always watching other people's lives on it at home.

DOT: You're talking about influencers presumably?

NEIL: Yah, that's it. Try yoga before breakfast - make some cushions out of old dresses - take hours to wrap your Christmas presents exactly the way I do, using old wallpaper that costs twenty pounds a roll anyway.

DOT: It's part of my job to keep up with the latest trends Neil.

NEIL: Trends. It's all been done before you know - most of it in the last war - but those poor sods did it out of necessity not for, some sort of shabby-chic effect. Anyway, shouldn't you be the one coming up with the ideas in the first place? You're just a bloody copycat.

DOT: Please Neil, don't go on about it. Look what we've got. Beautiful sunshine from morning to night, did you hear the birds this morning? And have you seen them in the evening, swooping down, almost touching the floor. They're like dive bombers, it's amazing.

NEIL: I heard that bloody Owl last night. How you can sleep through it I don't know - well actually I do - It'll be that vat of wine you're consuming every night. I assumed that extra case was full of clothes or shoes, no wonder it was so bloody heavy.

Muted laughter from the audience.

NEIL: What's so bloody funny about that?

DOT: What? I'm not laughing Neil - maybe you should have a glass or two tonight yourself - might chill you out a bit.

NEIL: Chill me out? I'm perfectly relaxed thank you very much. I would just like the option of watching the news - see what's going on in the world.

DOT: Neil - you're sitting there, on what must be the hottest day of the year so far, in full length trousers, a buttoned-up shirt and a baseball cap that's too big for your head.

NEIL: Like I said, I'm perfectly comfortable. You could do with something decent on top yourself, now you come to mention it. What is that a t-shirt?

DOT: Yes, I dampened it and twisted it tight - keeps my boobs cool and I want a tan without strap lines. I didn't think of packing a bikini either, so these lacy knickers are the next best thing.

NEIL: Might as well be nude!

DOT: Well why not? There's nobody for miles Neil. In fact.

NEIL: What the hell are you doing Dot. Okay, I get the point ... that T-shirts wet my trousers now and you won't get those knickers back - there stuck up in that tree branch, look.

Laughter from the audience.

HASANI: Hello?

DOT: Shit, there's someone over there, walking towards us from the woods ...

Laughter from the audience.

NEIL: Christ ... Quick get inside for god's sake. Stupid bloody woman.

Muted laughter from the audience.

HASANI: Hello.

NEIL: Who the hell are you?

HASANI: My name is Hasani. In Swahili it means handsome.

98.

NEIL: Does it now. Well you can cer i grafu.

HASANI: Sorry?

NEIL: In English that means go and ...

DOT: Neil!

Muted laughter from the audience.

DOT: Don't be so rude. Hello I'm Dot.

NEIL: Oh, found a dressing gown then?

HASANI: Hello Dot. My name is Hasani. In Swahili it means ...

NEIL: Can you stay at a safe distance please; you're getting too close!

DOT: For god's sake Neil, we're outside. I'm guessing you're not from the village.

NEIL: Racist.

Uncomfortable laughter from the audience.

HASANI: Correct Dot. I have lost my party fellows. We are a small community staying at a commune approximately thirty kilometres that way. We were foraging when I lost the others.

DOT: Thirty kilometres? That will take you hours.

HASANI: That is correct.

DOT: It'll be dark before you get back there.

HASANI: That is also correct.

NEIL: Well there we are then, everybody's clear on that. Now if you don't mind Mr. Biryani ...

HASANI: Hasani.

Uncomfortable laughter from the audience.

NEIL: I'd like to get back to ...

DOT: Neil! - A word - inside please. Hasani, please excuse me and my husband for a moment - I'll be right back.

HASANI: Very good Dot.

Neil and Dot disappear into the cabin

NEIL: He's not staying here! I mean look at him, he looks like he's just fallen off the circus train. What's with the colourful baggy trousers and seventeenth century military tunic, and what's all that stuff painted on his face?

DOT: He's a fellow human being, that's got no chance of getting back to his commune by nightfall. He's staying!

NEIL: What makes you think you've got the right to ...

DOT: This was my dad's cabin. He stays.

NEIL: What about the virus Dot? He's obviously got no hand sanitizer or mask in that carpet bag of his.

DOT: We'll spend the evening outside - around a fire - and he'll sleep in the bathroom. I'll wash it down tomorrow morning after he leaves.

HASANI: I have caused much disruption here. I will be on my way going.

DOT: No Hasani, you are welcome to stay.

NEIL: In the bathroom over there.

DOT: If that's okay?

NEIL: Until the morning.

DOT: Yes, until the morning.

HASANI: This is most excellent; I thank you a thousand times.

That evening Neil bangs the T.V. inside the cabin, trying to get some sort of signal while Hasani cooks a soup on the fire outside, watched over by Dot holding salt and pepper in one hand and a large glass of wine in the other.

DOT: Will you have a glass Hasani?

HASANI: Thank you, no. I don't ingest alcohol.

DOT: Neil?

NEIL: What?

DOT: Will you have a glass of white?

NEIL: Yes, actually I will.

Neil joins the other two.

HASANI: You are angry always Neil?

DOT: Yes.

NEIL: No, not at all. I would just like to watch the news. on a machine in there - it's called a television.

Uncomfortable laughter from the audience.

DOT: Neil! Pack it in!

HASANI: I know it. I used to be repairman.

NEIL: What?

HASANI: Yes. I can repair for you, unless it ken-ackered.

DOT: Ha, ha!

HASANI: I go now. Please watch foraged mushroom soup. Did you turn it off and on-again Neil?

DOT: Ha, ha, ha!

Laughter from the audience.

101.

NEIL: Don't laugh at that – it's not funny.

DOT: Is the T.V. really that important to you Neil?

NEIL: I simply want to find out how things are - out there.
DOT: To be honest with you - I'm starting to care less and less myself.

NEIL: I bet they're still showing those bloody adverts constructed solely of mobile phone footage and those smug basterds that give an interview with copies of their own book, strategically placed on the bookshelves behind them. Tossers!

DOT: I remember my father doing that. He was interviewed for a South Bank Show special when I was small.

NEIL: A special?

DOT: Yah, the whole show dedicated to his writing, with all his books on the shelf behind him. And do you know, I just can't see the appeal. I never could take to his writing - I always found it outdated, even years ago. It's misogynistic and inconsistent. Was that paragraph a joke, irony or just a semi-humorous recollection without a punchline? The male protagonist that dad came up with was rough, tough, and a sexy cliché - why do men think they know what turns women on anyway?

The character was all the things *he* wasn't.

NEIL: Or the things I'm not. I thought you were immensely proud of your father's books.

DOT: I'm proud of the fact that so many others enjoy his books - just not me I'm afraid.

NEIL: Well - fuck-a-duck!

Uncomfortable laughter from the audience.

DOT: Neil!

NEIL: What?

DOT: For Christ sake - stop being so crude - what's got into you?

Hasani returns, holding a piece of paper.

HASANI: I am mostly sorry Neil.

NEIL: I knew it – bloody useless.

DOT: Neil!

HASANI: No Dot, Neil is correct. It is without use - in fact once I opened the back of the television, I could see nothing. There were none of the electrical components inside - just this piece of paper with a child's drawing on it.

NEIL: Let me see?

DOT: What is it Neil - it's not one of mine I'm sure.

NEIL: I like it. I think it's one of your dad's little jokes. A small plant growing out of a pot.

DOT: What's it say - there?

NEIL: 'Stop watching the news and build a garden.'

Neil seems captivated with the drawing and studies it until Hasani passes him a bowl of mushroom soup.

HASANI: Please Neil, try some. It's good.

NEIL: Yes, it is. Thank you.

DOT: Might sober you up a bit.

NEIL: You what ...

HASANI: Neil, what is your profession please?

NEIL: I'm a Scientist Hasani.

DOT: Lab Assistant.

NEIL: A Histologist to be precise. I study the micro-anatomy of cells, tissues and organs.

DOT: You don't study them, Callahan does.

NEIL: Well - I prepare tissue samples for the pathologist to study. I am however specially trained to cut samples from organs - or other pieces of tissue - and stain them with materials such as dyes, which can aid in microscopic tissue analysis. A very important job at this particular time, I'm sure you'll agree Hasani?

HASANI: Yes. You will therefore be returning to your important work very soon, yes?

DOT: He's had you there.

NEIL: I've been working solidly since I graduated Dot.

HASANI: You are a scholar Neil. And I think - a gentleman.

DOT: I have a degree too Hasani.

NEIL: Huh!

DOT: What the hell is that for Neil?

NEIL: Well - an art degree is a little different from a science degree don't you think Hasani?

HASANI: I knew you were an artist Dot. I could see it when I first arrived here.

NEIL: You could see everything she had when you arrived mate.

Laughter from the audience.

DOT: I worked bloody hard for my B.A. as you well know Neil. You said you were proud of me when I graduated.

NEIL: I was - but I'm just stating facts - a science degree requires - by its nature - a more academic mind-set.

Hasani wonders off towards his bag just inside the cabin.

DOT: Okay - if that's true then why do I make more money than you?

Oooh ... from the audience.

NEIL: Oh yah ... yah. I'll tell you why - it's because your bloody industry has a completely disproportional sense of its own importance. Six-hundred quid for a bloody shop sign design - it's immoral.

DOT: At least I'm leaving my mark. All you do is obsess over dead cells and ...

NEIL: What's that noise?

DOT: Sounds like ...

NEIL: Oh no - it's not that bloody clapping for careers lot - it wouldn't carry all the way out here surely.

Uncomfortable laughter from the audience.

DOT: No - it's not. It's Hasani - look.

Hasani walks towards Neil and Dot banging on a small drum with what looks like a large turkey leg bone.

NEIL: Hasani - what the hell are you doing?

HASANI: It is an ancient instrument made from skin and bone.

NEIL: Sounds like it.

Muted laughter from the audience.

HASANI: Bronze age people kept human remains and used them as ornaments and musical instruments. The ancients will help to relax you both.

NEIL: Christ!

DOT: Well I think it's time I turned in.

NEIL: Yes.

Hasani stops playing.

HASANI: I would like to thank you for most welcome hospitality. I will leave early in morning, so I bid you farewell - now.

DOT: You are most welcome Hasani - and you must come back if you can't find your friends, isn't that right Neil?

NEIL: Yes. Yes of course.

CHAPTER 3
(JULY 2020)

Dot is on her own at the cabin.

DOT: Where the hell is he? Three and a half hours now - I know the village is twenty-odd miles away - but still ... What could be taking him so long?

Not long after, Neil arrives in the car. Dot helps with the noisy gate.

DOT: Where the hell have you been all this time Neil? And what on earth are you wearing?

NEIL: Put the kettle on love - I'll tell you all about it once I've sat down for a minute.

Neil sits on the chairs outside the cabin while Dot brings out some Tea.

DOT: So?

NEIL: There's nobody left Dot.

DOT: What does that mean? - I don't understand.

NEIL: The village - Wolves Hill - it's deserted. There's no one there anymore - not a sole.

Arrr ... from the audience.

DOT: What? ... Well ... What does it mean Neil?

NEIL: I don't know love. I got to the shop and thought, alright the lad is probably having a sneaky fag out the back or something. But once I'd got all we wanted and called out a few times - well it became evident that no bugger was there.

DOT: Did you knock on some of the doors - or try the garage?

NEIL: Yes of course. I walked the length of the village. The shop - the garage - the houses - the vicarage and then the chapel.

DOT: And no one?

NEIL: No one. The chapel had large boxes with loads of stuff - like a ... what-you-call-it ... a bring-and-buy sale thing ...

DOT: A jumble sale.

NEIL: Yes! But there was food and other stuff as well as clothes - the car's full of it - I grabbed anything I thought would be useful.

DOT: No T.V. though?

NEIL: Ah ... Shit. I didn't think of that. I could have got one from any of the houses.

DOT: You can't just take someone's T.V. Neil.

NEIL: There's nobody there Dot. The village is deserted I tell you.

DOT: Did you leave money - in the shop?

NEIL: No.

DOT: You should've left a note at least.

NEIL: What's the point - they've all gone!

DOT: Where?

NEIL: I don't know! - I'm going to get the stuff from the car.

Neil removes the items from the car and arranges them into piles of type on the grass, close to the cabin.

DOT: Neil - what the hell is this?

NEIL: It's a dress - I got it for you - nice isn't it?

DOT: It's a bloody wedding dress.

Muted laughter from the audience.

108.

NEIL: What? Well I don't know do I - thought it looked nice that's all.

DOT: Christ - how much wine have you got?

NEIL: You said get a months' worth - and since I've been having the odd glass ...

DOT: Bottle ...

NEIL: Or two, I thought it would be a good idea to stock up.

DOT: Nothing to do with the fact that you didn't have to pay for any of it at the time then?

NEIL: Look - if they've cleared out - for whatever reason - then some passing van driver will fill his boots anyway - and besides they'll have insurance to cover it - mind you, nothing was locked.
I did the same with the petrol - filled it up. It's nothing you wouldn't have done Dot.

DOT: I just can't get my head around the ...

NEIL: Shush! - Hear that?

DOT: What?

NEIL: Like a distant buzzing ... It's gone. No - there it is - listen.

DOT: What is that Neil?

NEIL: Two-stroke engine I reckon - and it's getting closer.

DOT: Oh god - here ...

NEIL: What are you giving me the teapot for?

DOT: A weapon!

Laughter from the audience.

NEIL: Don't be bloody stupid – you're showing yourself up woman - hand me that axe from over there!

Neil and Dot keep a close eye on the narrow path that leads to the noisy gate. The sound gets louder until a small motorbike comes into view with a very thin, half naked and dishevelled figure riding it, without a helmet.

DOT: Oh my god - it's Hasani!

The couple run over to open the gate, Neil dropping the axe. Hasani comes to a stop and topples over along with the bike to the ground.

DOT: My god - look at the state of him Neil.

NEIL: Let's get him inside.

Dot provides Hasani with a hot, sweet cup of tea while Neil gets a blanket and covers up his skinny but still muscular naked top half.

NEIL: What happened to you Hasani?

DOT: Christ Neil - give the man a chance ...

HASANI: No Dot - it is fine - I must tell you. When I left your hospitality, I returned to the commune to find no one there.

DOT: That was - four weeks ago.

HASANI: Yes, indeed Dot. I waited a week for my friends to return but nothing. I found a television and radio in another part of the area - used for office purposes I'm thinking. The reports were truly terrible - there had been a massive surge in the pandemic - thousands were dying every day - and then it stopped. Just stopped.

DOT: What do you mean - stopped.

HASANI: The prime minister was wishing all people well luck - and then nothing - anywhere - it all just stopped Dot.

DOT: My god Neil - what does it mean?

NEIL: It certainly explains why the village is empty - I suppose.

DOT: Explains what - I don't understand. Neil where are all the people?

110.

NEIL: Dying or dead in a make-shift hospital ward presumably Dot! Sorry love. There is a Medical Centre close to Wolves Hill, Wolves Valley I think it's called - but I wouldn't want to get anywhere near, at the moment.

DOT: My mother - and sisters.

Ahhh ... from the audience.

NEIL: Dot - I'm truly sorry. But it wouldn't do us any good, going back now.

Neil comforts Dot with a touch of her shoulder as he guides Hasani into the cabin.

HASANI: We should swap your car for a much larger vehicle at the village - and search for more survivors.

NEIL: I understand where you're coming from Hasani - but we know that we are safe here. If this thing is so contagious - why would we go looking for it? Presumably it will live outside the body for some time - but I do agree, we should get a better vehicle, wiped down before we use it of course.

HASANI: I can go to the village – find us such a vehicle and load it up with all fresh goods ...

NEIL: Before they go bad ... yes.

HASANI: I will take some of the goods back to the commune - so time will irradiate any virus left on them.

NEIL: That's sounds good - yes. I have some new clothes for you Hasani - they might be a little big, but never-the-less.

Within the hour, Hasani was dressed and ready to leave for the village using Neil and Dot's car. Neil offered Dot some food, which she declined, opting instead for wine.

NEIL: Here you go love - hasn't had much chance to chill yet I'm afraid.

DOT: It's fine, thanks. - What's the plan Neil?

NEIL: Well, Hasani wanted to leave - look for others - but I suggested sitting tight - for now at least and while we still have access to supplies from the village. He's getting a van or something of a similar size so we can limit our visits - in case the virus is present in the village.

DOT: He should scrub down when he comes back. And we should burn his clothes.

NEIL: What? A hot wash will do just fine Dot.

DOT: So, heat will kill it?

NEIL: About sixty to seventy degrees I reckon - should kill it. Put the clothes out in the sun all day - that'll do it for sure.

DOT: So, the sun kills it.

NEIL: Prolonged exposure to the sun should kill it - but without any new information - I don't know.

DOT: We need that T.V. then - or a Radio at least. Worth another trip to the village don't you think.

NEIL: I was thinking - just now. Hasani said the T.V. and Radio went dead. We'll pick up a T.V. next time we need to go to the village. My main concern now is water and electricity mains.

DOT: Oh my God!

It's late when Hasani arrives back from the commune, via the village. His shirt has fresh blood on it and his knuckle is cut. A rather drunk Dot fetches the First Aid box and slowly cleans it up. Neil has already gone to bed.

HASANI: I can do it Dot - if you wish?

DOT: Oh ... Bollocks. I'm perfectly capable of cleaning up a bit of blood. How'd you do it anyway.

HASANI: A door slammed onto my hand. The clothes that Neil give me are very big for my middle - they fall down - at same time as door slammed.

DOT: Ooh ... Matron!

HASANI: Why you laugh? What is Matron?

DOT: Nothing Hasani - don't you take any notice of me tonight. I think I better get off to bed. Ooh ... Bed!

Dot stubbles as she gets up, spilling her remaining wine and having to be steadied by Hasani, who's trousers fall down to the floor as a result. He is wearing no underwear.

DOT: Ooh ... It's happened again ... look!

HASANI: I am very sorry Dot.

DOT: Don't be Hasani - really don't be.
Hasani picks up his trousers and with one hand helps Dot into the cabin. He then retires for the night in the outside bathroom.

NEIL: Dot? What you doing in hear?

DOT: I thought it was time to share a bed again Neil.

NEIL: Is Hasani back?

DOT: Yes ... yes - he's very resourceful - and clever. I saw ... Ooh ... Matron!

Laughter from the audience.

NEIL: Oh god – not now – I'm tired. And you're drunk - and you stink of smoke and wine.

DOT: Yes ... Yes, I am - I do - but that has no insignificance to what I am - doing - with - wanting - in bed - trousers down - nice big ...

Laughter from the audience.

NEIL: For god sake – it's like a bloody kinder garden around here. Sorry Dot - you can't stay hear - I'm not ready yet. Let me help you to the other bedroom.

CHAPTER 4
(AUGUST 2020)

The next morning, Hasani had visited the commune to get supplies. Now it was Neil's turn to visit the village for the same. Dot and Hasani are sunbathing on the grass.

DOT: God it's hot. You don't mind if I take some of these stuffy clothes off do you Hasani?

HASANI: I am happiest when I am – as our god would have created us.

Hasani proceeds in taking of all his clothes and lies back down on the grass.

HASANI: You are happy with pants and T-shirt?

DOT: No actually I'm not, but I better wait for Neil first.

HASANI: You are a good and loyal wife Dot – and I think a talented artist.

DOT: Huh! I'm afraid I lost the passion some years ago Hasani. Although this does remind me of Art College.

HASANI: You smoked marijuana at the College?

DOT: Yes.

HASANI: I have some in my bag – lots growing all around the commune.

Hasani puts together a large joint. While Dot changes her mind on the nude sunbathing.

DOT: What the hell – you live once, right Hasani?

HASANI: Right on Dot. – Dot?

DOT: Yes.

HASANI: Do you worry about Neil sometimes – with him talking to himself?

114.

DOT: What – no – that's just his way, he's always done it. I think.

HASANI: But he tells people off – that aren't there. Could it be suffering from illness in his brain?

DOT: Defiantly not Hasani. He just finds it difficult dealing with – well most other people actually.

Neil returns to find his wife and Hasani sunbathing - nude and sharing a large joint.

NEIL: Is that a sodding Reefer?

DOT: For Christs sake Neil - nobody calls it that anymore. take your clothes off and have some.

NEIL: Where the hell did you get it from?

HASANI: There are many plants growing at the commune Neil. It is very old.

NEIL: Ancient shit - I suppose.

Muted laughter from the audience.

DOT: Neil …

HASANI: No - just old.

Hasani and Dot giggle. Dot stands and wraps a thin blanket around her well-tanned body and follows Neil into the cabin where he starts putting the supplies away.

NEIL: I assume all this nakedness will stop when winter comes - or are you both going to parade about inside the cabin with everything swaying about.

Muted laughter from the audience.

DOT: We've talked about this haven't we Neil. We could be the last - the only ones left. In the county - the country - shit maybe even the world. like Adam and Eve in our very own Garden of Eden.

NEIL: And what am I - the apple or the snake? – Nothing? – That was funny.

DOT: You could be God.

NEIL: How stoned are you Dot? Or have you changed - that much?

DOT: You're right about one thing - I'm not who I used to be Neil. - I miss Helen - you know our next-door neighbour - Helen. I suppose she's dead along with the rest.

NEIL: Most probably, yes. - Look, what do think about creating some sort of memorial - for the one's we've lost.

DOT: That's a really nice idea Neil.

Dot wraps her arms, and the thin blanket, around her husband. Pushing her naked body up against his clothes.

DOT: Wanna do it?

NEIL: Yes - in the woods.

DOT: Ooh ... Now?

NEIL: No, not now. We're going to need a decent location, somewhere flat, and tools for the job. It will need planning you know. Future generations might look upon it as a new world relic.

DOT: Where are the future generations going to come from Neil - where?

Dot backs away from Neil and closes the blanket once more.

NEIL: I think I saw a figure through the trees on the way to the village earlier.

Ooh ... from the audience.

DOT: You saw what?

NEIL: A person - maybe.

DOT: Well did you stop - call out to them - beep the bloody horn. Did they see you - what?

NEIL: I thought I was experiencing a hallucination.

DOT: Neil! What the hell is wrong with you? You're so anal about stacking the wood and all tins must be in order of use by date - you're a bloody drip Neil. And when you see someone - another actual human being - you fucking ignore it!

Oooh ... from the audience.

HASANI: Dot! please stop. you really shouldn't talk to husband this way - he is a good man - yes?

DOT: Yes. I'm sorry Neil. It's just sometimes I ...

NEIL: I know, so does he - and you haven't changed all that much after all.

A week later, all three companions are sitting around the camp-fire. Neil's pair of Y-fronts the only clothing on display.

DOT: It's decided then. For the sake of the human race - and until - or if - we find any other survivors, we shall try for a baby. We need to know you are happy about this Neil.

NEIL: Happy? Of course I'm not bloody happy about it.

DOT: Like you said, we can't artificially inseminate without the correct instruments or environment - can we?

NEIL: No.

DOT: And it could be the only way forward - couldn't it?

NEIL: Yes.

Hasani lets out a sudden loud yelping chant, which he achieves by vibrating his togue very quickly with his face to the night sky.

HASANI: You are a selfless man Neil. A warrior - and leader of our tribe. We will celebrate now with markings and dancing.

DOT: Hasani why are you cutting your arm with the knife - stop it!

NEIL: It' a ritual Dot.

HASANI: Correct again Neil.

117.

Hasani takes blood from the knife wound and marks himself, then the married couple with an upside-down 'V' on each forehead. He says a few words in Swahili and leaves the couple to check on the food that's cooking in the cabin.

DOT: You Okay Neil?

NEIL: Fine. I've seen these marks before you know. Five years ago - at work. Three murder victims, all with the same markings, in the same position too - in their own blood.

DOT: Neil ... You said you were fine with this - you're over-reacting. It's a common symbol - you'd probably see it everywhere if you looked for it - it's the universal symbol for the feminine.

Hasani approaches with an evening meal in tow.

NEIL: It's the masculine actually.

DOT: Sorry?

NEIL: The symbol is for the masculine - isn't that right Hasani?

HASANI: It would depend on which way you viewed it Neil.

118.

CHAPTER 5
(SEPTEMBER 2020)

Dot and Neil are outside, again enjoying a pleasant autumn evening by the fireside while Hasani prepares a meal in the cabin.

NEIL: All I'm saying is - why do you have to make so much noise, Hasani doesn't. What do you think it's like for me - to be out hear knowing what you two are doing in there? I know you're getting more like Hasani – with all the African stuff and all - but what's with the sudden screaming like that - you never did that when we ...

Muted laughter from the audience.

DOT: I'm sorry Neil. I'll keep it down in future.

NEIL: Good. It's disturbing.

DOT: You do know Neil don't you - that you're going to be just as much a father to any child we're blessed with, as Hasani will be.

NEIL: Yes – that would be nice.

DOT: Oh Neil. Do you really believe we might be the only ones left?

NEIL: On the planet - no - but on Cloverdragon, maybe.

DOT: So, what difference will a child really make?

NEIL: You're asking me that now? Look it would bide us time if nothing else.

DOT: Time for what?

NEIL: Time to find another tribe. One that our child would someday join with and produce another and so on.

DOT: And if there is, no other tribe?

NEIL: Then we must have more children until there is at least one of each sex.

DOT: Eew - Neil! That's incest!

NEIL: No - that's survival.

The end of the month approaches. Neil returns with the monthly stock-up from the village. When he arrives Dot and Hasani are nowhere to be found. He hears excited voices coming from the outside bathroom-come old shipping container. He finds a crack in the casing and peers inside. Shocked and angered at what he sees he waits outside the bathroom until Dot and Hasani come out.

DOT: Neil, when did you ...

NEIL: Didn't hear me did you.

DOT: What's wrong?

NEIL: What's wrong? I might have only got a 2.1. Dot, but even I know that you cannot get pregnant - orally.

Uncomfortable laughter from the audience.

Neil makes a fist and violently grunts at it.

HASANI: We thought we would try it with water - the shower you know, but ...

NEIL: How much of an idiot do you really think I am. It's over - do you both hear me - the experiment is over!

DOT: Yes - yes, it is - I think I'm pregnant.

Cheers from the audience.

120.

CHAPTER 6
(JUNE 2021)

Baby is born. Neil and Hasani help with the birth, which went well. Both mother and child are healthy.

HASANI: You are a very special lady Dot - we make a beautiful baby.

Arrr ... from the audience.

DOT: Yes - he is beautiful, isn't he?

NEIL: He looks like a Winston - or a Neil. First man on the moon and all that, poignant don't you think?

DOT: We thought - Adam.

NEIL: Oh god - a bit obvious, isn't it?

HASANI: Adam is good Neil. 'A' for Adam - maybe one day we get to 'H' for Hasani.

NEIL: You're having a laugh ...

Muted laughter from the audience.

DOT: Let's just take one thing at a time shall we boys? I'm certainly in no rush to go through anything like that again.

NEIL: Absolutely. You did amazingly love - I'm very proud of you.

Later that day, Hasani is preparing food in the cabin, while Neil, Dot and baby Adam enjoy the weather that summer brings.

NEIL: Have you noticed any changes in Hasani recently Dot?

DOT: No - not really.

NEIL: You haven't noticed that his accent has dropped considerably since we first met last year?

DOT: He's very intelligent Neil. He has adopted the English language very well and we should be pleased with ourselves for that.

NEIL: Well, I could have sworn that I heard a bit of scouse - when you were giving birth, he nearly passed out you know.

DOT: Yes - I know what you mean. The odd word can sound a bit Liverpudlian, especially when ... well ... let's just say, he reaches his most - emotional moments.

NEIL: I was thinking that it might be time I tried to reach that Medical Centre at Wolves Valley - or even Wool Pit, the next village along, see what I can find.

DOT: Oh god - do you think it's safe - and why now? The summers here and we've got everything we need Neil.

NEIL: Well, I wasn't going to say anything but the flour, we used at the beginning of the week, was the last in our stock.

DOT: Why didn't you say?

NEIL: I didn't want to worry you, so late in the pregnancy. And anyway, my plan was to raid the kitchens in the houses, must be loads of flour in them, collectively.

DOT: Oh, you mean the houses that you won't go in - the houses that obviously creep you out - otherwise we would have a T.V., and probably a DVD player, in the cabin by now.

NEIL: It's true - to an extent. The place is weird, bloody crows everywhere and things flapping in the wind. It makes you jump when you're on your own, you know.

DOT: That's your problem Neil, you don't say anything - especially if it involves fear.

NEIL: It's not fear - I've never been afraid of anything ...

DOT: And there it is - exactly my point.

NEIL: I'm not scared Dot.

DOT: I know, but next time I want to come with you. We might even find some baby clothes somewhere.

NEIL: Okay, but just you - right?

DOT: Yes. It'll be nice for just us, to do something together for a change. Hasani can stay here with Adam.

A week later, Neil and Dot arrive at Wolves Hill Village. It is just how Neil described.

DOT: What's that smell?

NEIL: I don't know. I have noticed it before, but it wasn't as strong then - thought it was the rubbish bins to be honest.

DOT: It's coming from over there - carried on the wind. Eew!

NEIL: That's the Chapel, where I said the Jumble sale stuff was. Put you're mask on; it will help with the smell.

DOT: Oh good. There's bound to be baby-grows at a Jumble. Oh ... will they be safe for Adam?

NEIL: By now ... certainly, yes, we'll wash them anyway.

The large room has mold-ridden baked goods on plates, boxes of once-fresh and tinned goods, and piles of clothes, now dampened with slightly browned whites from the winter conditions. The next smaller room, that lead from the larger, has unfinished pints of beer and other drinks, as well as un-eaten sandwiches, chicken drumsticks and sausage rolls.

NEIL: What the hell?

DOT: Looks like they were having a party.

NEIL: Well - it was cut short by something. Or someone.

DOT: I can't believe how bad that food stinks. It doesn't even look that decayed. Oh Neil ... don't smell it.

NEIL: It's not the food Dot. The smells coming from behind that big velvet curtain over there. Wait ... when you see it move with the breeze ... there see ... now ...

DOT: Eew! Your right, there's something rotten behind it.

They both approach cautiously. Neil slowly peels back the heavy curtain as they both cover their masked mouths and noses with hands. In the cavernous space lies the bodies of twenty to thirty dead bodies.

Neil steadies Dot with a tight grip to her arm as she lets out a brief but intense scream.

Gasps from the audience.

DOT: Oh my god - it's like those photographs from the Nazi death camps.

NEIL: Yes. They're all piled up on top of each other.

DOT: Neil – are you smiling?

NEIL: No Dot – I'm grimacing.

DOT: It's horrific Neil. Who could have done this? Oh shit - that one is looking at me ... look!

NEIL: Well I can tell you one thing for certain Dot. They've been murdered.

DOT: Murdered - by who?

NEIL: Look at these marks - they're a bit faded now - but look ...

DOT: I don't want to Neil.

NEIL: You must ... Look ... four ... five ... six ... They all have it. An upside-down 'V' - in blood on their foreheads.

DOT: The symbol for the masculine ...

NEIL: The mark of Hasani!

Gasps from the audience.

Neil and Dot race back to the truck.

DOT: Oh my god ... Adam!

124.

NEIL: We're going to fill up with petrol - get back to the cabin - grab Adam and head off for Wool Pit, Liberty or even Jacqui's Town if we have to.

DOT: He wouldn't hurt Adam would he Neil? His own flesh and ...

NEIL: Don't worry, he has no idea that we know anything. You stay in the truck, after opening the gate for me, and I'll grab the baby. I bloody knew there was something up with that guy from day one.

DOT: Just be careful Neil - get us out of this.

NEIL: I will - don't you worry, everything's going to be alright.

Neil produces a large claw-hammer from the door bin on his side and puts it to sit in his lap as he drives back to the cabin at speed. Adam is on a blanket on the ground while Hasani is seen drying his hands in a towel, one of which he then uses to wave at the returning couple. His welcoming face drops when he sees Neil bounding towards Adam with the claw-hammer in hand.

HASANI: Neil ... What is all the goings on?

NEIL: Just stay right where you are Hasani - not another step, d'you here?

Neil lifts the baby from the blanket and back-steps towards the truck, it's engine still running and an anxious looking Dot inside.

HASANI: Hay ... Neil!

NEIL: I told you - stay where you are! You come any closer and I'll bash your bloody brains in Hasani!

Neil hands Adam to Dot through the open window of the truck and makes his way to the driver's side, hammer at the ready. Hasani starts to quicken his pace towards them as the truck, reverses back through the gate.

HASANI: Hay ... What the fuck d'you think your doin' man?

Gasps from the audience.

NEIL: Shit - did you hear that Dot?

DOT: Oh my god yes - a Liverpool accent.

NEIL: Oh Christ!

DOT: What is it Neil?

NEIL: He's behind us - on that bloody bike.

DOT: Oh no!

NEIL: It's okay Dot - it's only a two-stroke. He'll never keep up.

DOT: But when we get to Wolves whatever ...

NEIL: When he gets there after us - I'll be ready, don't you worry. I'm not going to let anything happen to either of you - I promise.

DOT: And I believe you. I've been so stupid Neil ...

NEIL: No time for that now Dot - just hold on tight, we've got onto the main road.

Once on the main road, that leads to the village and ultimately the next, Neil puts the 3.5 litre engine of the pick-up truck to use. The two-stroke motorbike carrying Hasani is reduced to a mere speck in Neil's mirror view. He slows to a sensible but progressive pace as he prefers to keep the speck in sight. They drive straight through the village of Wolves Hill, see a curious sign with an arrow which reads 'CORONAVIRUS VACCINATION - This way', and on towards the village of Wool Pit.

DOT: Neil ... There's a car coming in the opposite direction.

NEIL: You're right! We're saved Dot - there is life!

Cheers from the audience.

DOT: It's a Police car.

NEIL: We should stop - tell them about Hasani behind us.

DOT: No Neil ... please don't. Whoever they are, might have stolen the Police car and Hasani could catch up with us too quickly.

NEIL: Okay, I'll put my foot down then. If they are Police - they'll have to chase us to Wool Pit - we'll have an escort Dot. I will prove to you that I can do this.

DOT: Neil, you don't have to prove anything to me. I love you just the way you are, especially with Adam. I don't want anyone else anymore - just you. I know that now. So - floor it!

The Police car flashed its lights once on approach as the pick-up screamed passed it.

The lights were quickly accompanied by a loud siren as the Police car u-turned and gave chase. The two-stroke was now nowhere to be seen.

They reach Wool Pit and must slow down. Everything is normal. There are people going about their business as usual and the shops are open.
DOT: I can't believe it. All this time.

Orrr ... from the audience.

NEIL: I'll stop over there Dot. You get out with Adam and stand out-side that Fish N' Chip shop with those people. I'll talk to the Police and if Hasani turns up, well let's just hope he won't try anything with so many people about. Okay - go!

DOT: I love you Neil!

NEIL: Go!

The couple leave the pick-up at the same time, the Police quickly grabbing hold of Neil as he does so. The mask-wearing public start to gather to on-look.

NEIL: There's a guy pursuing us - he's a killer. He murdered a load of villagers at Wolves Hill and hid their bodies in the back-room of the Chapel. There he is now - on the bike!

One of the Police Officers stands out into the road and holds up a hand, stopping the bike before it's gets too close to Neil. Hasani steps off, throwing the bike to the ground and trying to push past the Officer in his way.

HASANI: Arrest that man - he kidnapped my son!

Boos ... from the audience.

NEIL: You're a murderer!

HASANI: You what?
Another Police car turns up, as well as a van with several Police Officers spilling out, dividing themselves between Neil and Hasani. Dot moves away from the Fish N' Chip Shop and gets as close to Neil as the Police will allow.

DOT: My husband is right. That man is a killer and a fraud!

HASANI: Dot ... I don't know what he has gotten into your head ...

DOT: Oh yah ... well how come you suddenly sound like Ringo then? He told me he was from Africa.

HASANI: Actually ... I never did. You just assumed it, racist bitch!
Muted boos from the audience.

NEIL: What did you say?

Neil tries to break through the Police Officers to get to Hasani. They react by putting each man in separate Police vehicles. Dot talks to a senior Police Officer.

DOT: It's true - what my husband says. There's a pile of dead bodies at the Chapel in Wolves Hill village - and you'll probably find more at a commune he visited about thirty kilometres north of Devil's Head Lake - we never went there.

The senior Police Officer assures her that once a statement has been taken, from all involved, her and her husband will be released. Dot and Adam are last to leave the scene in yet another Police vehicle.

Applause and cheers from the audience.

CHAPTER 7
(JULY 2021)

Neil and Dot have returned to their house in Michael's Town.

Lockdown is over.

DOT: Neil ... What the hell are you doing with that chainsaw?

NEIL: I'm going to do something I should've done a long time ago - cut that bloody bush down!

Muted laughter from the audience.

DOT: Oh god ...

Dot is interrupted by knocking at the door. She answers it.

DOT: Helen ... God it's good to see you, come on in.

HELEN: I heard about what happened up at Devils Head Lake Dot. You must have been terrified.

DOT: How did you ... Oh, of course. Your job.

HELEN: And who's this hansom little devil then?

DOT: Adam ... Meet your Aunty Helen.

HELEN: He's lovely Dot.

DOT: Born out of a newly requited love Helen.

HELEN: Things alright with you both now then?

DOT: Yah ... better than ever. It's just a shame that it took such a traumatic drama to get me to realize it.

HELEN: That's good. I'm happy for you - and you know I'm right here if you need to talk ...

DOT: Professionally?

HELEN: As a friend Dot. What's Neil up to next door?

DOT: Oh Christ ... he's gone round there. The bloody bush has been an issue for a couple of years, blocks the natural light into his study from midday on. Now, of course he's found the 'no nonsense' part of his psyche, so he's decided to chop it down. Gruff will throw a fit. Neil ... Neil!

HELEN: Of course, you wouldn't have heard.

DOT: Heard what?

HELEN: Gruff was found dead, must have been the day after you left last year.

The sound of the chainsaw gets louder as Neil hacks at the foundations of the bush with a viciously satisfying energy. The women have to raise their voices to be heard through the noise pulsing though the open kitchen window.

DOT: Oh no, not another victim of the virus?

HELEN: No, he was murdered. His nephew, from the farm you know, found him. I went in after I heard a call for help. The Police said afterwards that it was a robbery gone wrong, but I never believed that, like the stuff they didn't report in the paper.
As if killing the poor old sod wasn't enough, the sick bastards made a blood mark on his forehead in the shape of an upside-down 'V'.

END

ALL THIS TIME

BOTTLE IT

BOTTLE IT

ONE

Darkness falls as the young crowd are packed in tight at the Cellar Bar as the band are playing a 'Sting' cover and Kimona is knocking back her self-served drinks at a staggeringly fast rate. She finishes and finds a table to put the glass on before staggering out of the exit and into the beer garden where she begins to roll a cigarette. The fifty-two-year-old woman walks straight into two big girls, causing one to spill an amount of her drink on the floor.

"Orr, Sori boio, ydi na fi?"(welsh) - "Orr, sorry mate, was that me?"

"I don't know what the fuck you just said, but you owe me a pint!" Said one of the big girls with an aggressive scowl.

"Rwy'n sori bois ond gwariais I popeth heno, prynodd chi un amser eto oright?"(welsh) - "I'm sorry mate but I'm all spent out tonight, I'll get you one next time alright?"

Kimona taps the girl on the shoulder and walks out of the beer garden onto the street, attempting to light her cigarette as she goes. The last drink has its effect as she walks through various streets semi-visually observing the night-life and occasionally commenting, particularly on the female contingent, to herself. She comes to the end of her cigarette and puts it out with her good foot and as she is close to home, she produces a large bunch of keys from her pocket and is now clumsily sorting one apart from the rest. Suddenly there is a piercing voice a couple of yards behind her,

"I think you forgot something didn't you - mate?"

Kimona turns around and strains to focus on the two figures walking towards her at a heavy pace. It's the big girls from the bar who must have followed her home.

"Helo eto, beth rydyn ni'n anghofio?"(welsh) - "Oh, hello again, what did I forget?" Kimona swayed as she attempted to stand up straight, her just about five-foot height dwarfed by the other women, aided by high

heels, as they reach her position.
"Your manners - you black bitch!"

The gobby one hits her - hard - and a few times more from both once she's on the ground.
When Kimona comes to - she picks up her keys and limps the short way home, holding her injured arm against her chest. She navigates the extremely hazardous twisted old slate staircase down to her basement flat, with the ease of experience. Keys - door open - in - door closed - drink poured - sit down - drink - sleep. Another day in Paradise – done.

It's early afternoon - who knows what day of the week - Kimona is sober. The basement flat is tidy, if you take the empties out of the scene. She refers to it as her bucker, which it resembles due mostly to its low ceilings. The flat consists of three rooms - a bathroom - the main living room with a sofa, a chair, TV, coffee table, shelves, impressive looking African Spear and Shield and posters: 'You're not a Nut, You're A Peach' - 'What if Your Right?' - 'UB40 Signed Off'. The bedroom leads directly to the kitchen, so: bed, cooker, linin basket, bin, chest of drawers with neatly stacked canned food on top. The walls have a neat row of framed certificates for long distant running. There's a back door which leads to a small ally-way, where the large lidded bins for the whole building are kept.
Kimona's furiously searching through cupboards, under the bed, and in the fridge for any remnants of alcohol. She holds each empty bottle she finds up to her eye, double checking there's nothing left. A dribble is enough to have her unscrew the lid and fling the bottle back - perfectly vertically - getting, literally, every drop out and into her dry mouth where it's absorbed under her tongue - most direct for effect.

The search continues outside, in the large dented wheelie bins - 'Dregs n' Drops' she chants to herself in a sort of panicked motivational way. Kimona feels her way around each bag in each bin - she knows instinctively if it's a booze bottle - she could probably tell you precisely which, along the alcohol content, if anyone ever asked, but this one felt different. She tears her neighbours' black bag carefully and eases out a large, bulbous bottle of what looked like some sort of liquor - the design was foreign - really foreign. Kimona couldn't make out even one legible letter, never mind a word.

"Oh well - what the hell." Kimona opened it up and took a quick sniff - strong stuff was the message to the brain - the bottle flies vertical. It was one good mouthful, sweet and herby and very strong. The warmth in her chest came first - she imagined any virus partials getting wiped out like the alien ships in a Space Invaders game - then the exhale and relaxation of the muscles in her neck and shoulders. The pleasure wave came last, in the form of head up to the sky, drooped eyelids and a small smile.
Once passed, Kimona takes another look at the unusual bottle.
"Nice that, I'll keep hold of it, I think. One bedside lamp coming up." Kimona was handy with things like that. She puts it down by her feet and returns to the bins, "Aha! Got one! Cooking Sherry," close to a third of a bottle left, "nice one." she says excitedly to herself as she puts the dried batter-mix-covered bottle into a plastic bag she has pulled from her pocket, then picks up the foreign looking bottle again.
A neighbours' net curtain twitched; Kimona shakes the bulbous bottle in the direction of the twitchy window.
"Hay don't fucking judge me bitch!" The neighbour lives a flat above her, has done since Kimona moved in. She's a cantankerous old crone - reminded Kimona of her Mamma, 'she was a bitch too.' She reminisced. 'But when she was nice - it was real nice you know? Not like the other girls' mums, all fake in front of others. No - Mammas nice was the best.'
Kimona, as a force of habit, unscrews the lid to check the bottle's empty and looks through it - her anger forcing the urge for a drink. It is - of course - empty, but she stays there.
The bottle distorts the scene in a sort of comfortable way and the slight colouring of the glass helps too.
"Lookin' at the world through Rose-coloured glasses, everything is Rosy now..." Her quiet singing is abruptly stopped by the sight of the neighbour checking once more from behind the net curtains, viewed by Kimona through the bottom of the bottle. Kimona sees her clearly - but what she sees looks - Alien. She quickly blinks and checks the window again from just above the bottle-neck - the neighbour is normal looking - back again through the bottle and there - it's a hideously ugly sight. The elderly neighbours' hair has gone, her eyes are circular and black, her mouth emotionless and small, with an upturned nose so severe that from that distance looks flesh-less.

"Fucking hell!" Kimona swiftly limps her way back to her flat, where she quickly clears the coffee table of empties and puts the foreign looking bottle slap-bang in the middle for further analysis while using a small glass to drink the remainder of the Cooking Sherry.

136.

TWO

Twenty-thirty.
In the last ten years we've seen thirteen serious outbreak spikes of the viruses Covid-19, 23 and most recently 28.
You can still smell the chlorine on everything from the last one, reminds me of the days when you could use a Swimming Pool.
Look at her, up there on the street - she's nice - long hair. Wig no doubt, nobody's got real long hair anymore - no Hairdressers to mess about with it. Most women cut their hair short at home with clippers, then buy a nice wig or two for appearances - but not me - keep it shaved nowadays. I used to sell it, good money too, but I won't let it grow long enough anymore - unhygienic. I do like her, couldn't get near it though, I'd like to get up real close too - who am I kidding? She wouldn't go near me! The ethnic risk factor - B.A.M.E. the media call it - Black, Asian and minority ethnic - bit of a broad term in my opinion, the term itself is segregational, inaccurate bullshit! Disproportionate numbers of deaths within the B.A.M.E. community. What community, there's no such thing anymore, be nice to find one though. Bet they've got communities in Jamaica - not much chance of me getting out there these days though. The government own the airlines and ships, so nobody gets out of the country without screening first and a huge pile of cash second. You can only drive if your car is electric, hard up urchins like me usually cycle, but I sold mine ages back when the buses still ran. Very little public transport now - prisoners and goods is what they're used for mostly.
I've got a message come through on my H.C. (Health Card) - it glows a illuminant green. - 'BETTERBUY - 06:00 - 10:00 - PLEASE RESPOND TO THIS MESSAGE WITHIN 1 HOUR TO CONFIRM YOUR SHIFT - BE SMART - STAY APART' - That's my next shift, could've been any number of retail places, it's designed to keep people from claiming Euro Universal Credit and an attempt to fix the mass unemployment figures. Brexit never materialized, especially after the formation of the E.E. - short for Eastern Empire, China, Japan, Korea, Hong Kong and Taiwan as well of a couple of other countries I can't remember or care about to be honest. It was formed to rival the U.S. Then Europe joined in and formed an Eastern and Western State. 'Stronger Together' was the big slogan.

It's all the same shit just under a different flag if you ask me, but who knows whether things would be better or worse, with or without unity. Five shifts a week at ten Euro's an hour, gets me eight hundred a month - shit I know - but this place is only two and a half – and it does me and the other urchins alright. I call my neighbours that because they are the forgotten – the people that literally have nothing. The council put us in hear to keep us off the streets and off their backs. Billy was the exception, he died last week – nice old boy, non-judgemental. He had been living here for years apparently – used to collect all the shit of the street that nobody else wanted. He owned his flat, but that didn't stop the them breaking their way in and rehousing him while they cleared the place out. They were going to send Billy back, once they finished, but he caught the virus and copped-it a day before. It all happened within a week – last week. They should off left him alone – bloody do-gooders killed him in the end.

Food is like a hundred or so and if you buy mostly cans it leaves me a decent amount for the nectar. Vodka's my favourite but I can't afford the proper stuff, might get a small bottle for my birthday if I manage to put some cash away - did that before and forgot where I put the bloody stuff - there's fifty E's hiding away somewhere in this flat. No, I drink 'Insane Vodca'. It's made from potatoes and they add sanitizer to it to increase the alcohol and - as the tag says - 'known to kill the Covid'.

Later that afternoon, Kimona is staring at the foreign looking bottle. She has picked it up several times but not had the courage to look though it again. The Cooking Sherry is wearing off, she'll have to spend her last twenty Euro wisely, it needs to last two days. Not easy when a bottle of 'Insane' costs eighteen and lasts about the same in time - a Euro an hour. There's a loud knock at the door, not three meters away from where Kimona is sitting.

She quickly slides from the sofa and shimmies along the floor towards the door. There's a small hole in the panel at the bottom which she has covered with a small piece of one-way-mirror, held in place with parcel tape on her side. 'Black shoes, trousers and clip board'. She acknowledges.

"Hello madam, we've come to collect moneys owed to the local council authority please. Hello? We know you're in there."

"Do I owe you money?" Kimona asked, still lying on the floor.

"Yes - well not me personally, but..." Came the voice from the other side.

"Well, what you doin' here then? Breakin' the law, that's what. Demandin' money from me, with menaces." The Caribbean accent gets stronger when Kimona is rattled.

"You owe Council Tax madam!"

"I know that, and I'm in dispute about that with the Council, which is my business and none of yours, but what I'm askin' you is - why are you breakin' the law of this land and askin' me for money, when I don't owe you any?"

"I represent a debt collection agency, who took on your dept and are therefore authorized to collect it - in full."

"You do realize that you are breakin' the law, don't you? This country's laws stipulates that for one person to demand money from another you must first have a written contract with that person - it's to stop a thing called demanding money with menses - and I do not have a contract with you or your company, therefore you need to jog-on!"

"I have, in my possession a court order signed by..."

Kimona slides back to the coffee table and grabs the foreign looking bottle. She unscrews the lid and positions herself as low as she can to try and get a head view of the debt collector. She does - and he is - one of them. Just as ugly as the old woman in the flat above - in fact the same face, made all the more horrifying by the closeness of the proximity this time. Kimona let out a short yelp, quickly muted by her own hand which dropped the bottle on the floor and forced her to bang her head on the bottom of the door.

"Are you alright in there madam? Would you like me to call for some assistance?"

Kimona just sat with her back against the door and both hands tightly wrapped around her mouth until she heard the debt collector assenting the steps to the street above.

I've gotta get out of here, before he comes back. I'll get some 'Insane' and hide out under the Jetty on the beach until late, hopefully there'll be no 'Waffles' hanging about.
'Waffles' or 'What the Fucks' are generally overweight smokers that don't care if they contract or spread the virus. The sub-culture is surprisingly strong in numbers, big enough in fact to keep the fast food chains open (as well as so called normal citizens sneaking in a cheeseburger now and then).

139.

They are ostracised like punks with their Mohikans were back in the late 1970's - people will move away from a 'Waffle' or overweight person because the chances of them being fatally affected by the virus is forty percent higher, apparently. True 'Waffles' are the new rebels so dress in biker or rock chick gear with the hardcore members riding red diesel fuelled motorbikes. They mostly hang-out in and around the old public buildings that serve no purpose anymore. Places I remember like the library. Green moss and various grasses now fill the non-repaired cracks in the walls with dust, rust and dirt almost covering the old paint work. My Mamma used to take me there when I was little, every Sunday without fail, now the buildings sheer presence seems to darken the sky above it. If I'd been fat enough when the 'Waffles' started, I might have joined them. They'd be alright if it weren't for the criminal element. The steeling, Bank and Post Office raids were alright, but once they started targeting old rich folks, raping, maiming and killing them in their own homes, was when they crossed the line for me.

Right - shoes on - twenty Euro - keys. Damn! I've knocked the bloody things behind the TV - hang on what's that? It's my birthday card, the last one I got from my Mamma - it's got the fifty Euros in it - nice one! That's it then, screw the Jetty, I'm off to the Pub for the night - wait –
I need my Health Card to get in.
Everyone's got one, a Health Card or H.C. as most call it. It includes a censor for detecting the past versions of the virus. If you want the most recent version, 28, it will cost you around five hundred. It's common place to test people you come into contact with - by holding the card up to their forehead for a second then the little read out, same as the one that told me about my shift tomorrow, tells you if they're pos or neg. And that's not all, you can get any sort of app you want on it, as long as you're willing to pay the price that is. It can test other people for drugs, alcohol, diabetes, some sexual transmitted diseases, even criminal records, although that one is illegal, but loads have it. They use it when they're on first dates or dancing with someone in a club, dads use it on their daughter's boyfriends for Christ sake. The card will also notify the authorities if you are more than twenty-five kilometres away from home during times of lockdown which are the highest peak times of the pandemic. Typically, August to July, every year so far.

"Get your hands off me you ape!" A doorman is escorting Kimona out of the Pub,

"I told you before - out!"

"What's your problem man? I've just been serving myself in there for over three hours now, causin' no trouble, stayin' at my table, stickin' to the rules - so what's up?"

"You were identified by a member of staff as the person who stole some fixtures from this Pub last month."

"It nuh true man!" Kimona's angry Caribbean was back, "Get yu 'ands off me man!"

The doorman looked puzzled and as a precaution kept her in a sort of headlock, her head fitting naturally under his arm due to their height difference.

"Yu arm green man," Kimona wriggled free, she was much stronger than she looked, "yu need fo guh bade." She was referring to his body odour.

The doorman pointed at Kimona, now standing on the street,

"Don't come back!"

"I bet you're one of them, aren't you," she pointed back, her accent switched to welsh, "one of those bloody aliens in it - I know - I'll be back to prove it too!"

Down the steps - key in lock - bottle grabbed - door slammed shut. The Pub was almost opposite Kimona's place, across the street and up a bit, so it took no time at all before she was back on street level again, spying on the Doorman via the bottle from the top of the treacherous steps.

"He's clean." She says quietly to herself and with a level of disappointment, although she didn't hate him – nice enough lad – just doing his job. And she had stolen the African Spear and Shield last month after all. Kimona moves down the street a little, keeping to her side, and views again. Same result ̄__ the Doorman is indeed human, but then two patrons exit the Pub, one man and a woman. They are both Alien. Kimona pushes her back against the wall behind her, not wanting to see but not wanting not to either. She lowers the bottle to her side as the couple stand in the street, the male lighting two cigarettes and handing one to the female before wondering off down towards the next street. Kimona walks back over towards the Doorman,

"OK, so you're clean, but those two who just left were..."

The Doorman instantly placed one foot back a step, an opened-palmed hand out towards Kimona and his other to his face, seemingly informing others of a clear and present danger.

"Please don't come any closer and put the bottle down!" He demanded loudly, his jaw the only part of him that moved.

"I'm trying to tell you that there is some weird shit going on round here, just take a look though the bottle at the punters in the Pub and you'll see what I mean, it can somehow reveal a person's true identity." She held the bottle with an outstretched arm towards the Doorman, she had slowed her approach but not stopped as demanded. "Just take a quick look, I know you're alright so I can trust you." She was now within reaching distance to the Doorman, who stood still as a statue, eyes fixed on Kimona's bottle. "I need somebody to verify..."

Suddenly the Doorman's arm sweeps across his body hurling the bottle out of Kimona's hand, his torso stopping dead once more as the move was executed.

The bottle hit the pavement without breaking and rolled up the incline before stopping and starting to roll back again. Kimona moved towards where the bottle might end up, leaving the Doorman frozen in his martial arts stance. She kept her eye on its trajectory until her view was blanketed by two young lads who had just left the Pub and were running up the street, one of them very skilfully intercepting the rolling bottle, volley-kicking it into the air and across the street until it landed against Kimona's own metal railings. It smashed into a thousand pieces, the boys cheered and chanted 'one-nil' as they continued upwards.

142.

THREE

     BetterBuy - 08:30 - Tea-break time - fifteen minutes. I have my flask - three parts strong black Coffee - two parts 'Insane Vodca' - thanks for the fifty Mamma.
I'm dying for a smoke, but I can't take the flask outside with me. Halfway through the shift and my fingers are already changing the colour of the gloves they've given us to wear. I'll have to ask for a new pair. The broken glass from the bottle cut up my fingers pretty good last night as I gathered all the pieces I could find off the pavement. They're currently piled on my Coffee table awaiting re-construction.
It always amazes me how many people still come along to the supermarket, I mean who the hell are they? Most people now work from home, so they get home delivery - twenty-four-seven. All manual maintenance work takes place at night, and under twelves are banned - since they found out that they are the main carriers of the latest strain - covid-28. So, who the hell are these people?
I've been on the veg all morning. It's weird - last time I was on veg it was all potatoes, onions and carrots. Now it's Peppers, coquettes and tomatoes. Vegetables are strictly seasonal now - have been for about two years - maybe that's who these shoppers are - picking the best of the bunch for themselves - vegetable vigilantes, or maybe cheating 'Les Naturals'. They're the sort of hippy, anti-pollution, environmental lot, fixed on the idea that the virus is nature's way of revenge. Every town has them. They grow their own hair, long, beards too and don't use any cosmetics or stuff like that, not even sanitary products for the ladies. Strangely enough they smell worse in the winter months than they do in the summer. The 'Les Naturals' will, or should, only eat what they can grow, and they recycle everything, even they're own shit and piss apparently. The piss is used to clean stuff and dye their hair, a lot of them are blond, and the shit is made into fuel and ovens. Each to their own is what I say.

I made a big mistake earlier whilst un-boxing the bell peppers - I tuned into the beeps. The beep that every item going through the bar-code scanner makes, if you tune into it - into them, there must be thousands of them a minute, it can send you crazy.

Every beep - more money spent. Money is like manure - when spread about, things grow. When it's hoarded, it stinks!

Oh, shit it's Meg, she's bound to keep me talking when all I want to do is finish my Coffee. She's alright though to be fair, at least she speaks to me - I see her a lot at various workplaces - works like a horse. Five kids - four now - lost her husband and eldest, he was a 'Waffle', to the virus poor cow. Here she comes - I would though - but then again, I would with anyone.

"Kimona... you alright?"

"Yah thanks Meg, you?"

"Oh, you know, mustn't grumble."

"Seeing anyone yet?" Kimona took a slurp of coffee from the flask cup and gave her best seductive eyes look.

"No, no time for that sort of thing these days."

"You should try, give yourself a break now and then - you can always come around my place - anytime - you know that right?"

"Yah, thanks Kimona, I appreciate that, thanks."

"No problem at all Meg - we could have a couple of glasses of wine or something one night - it is wine you like isn't it - I've seen you putting a good few bottles in the car haven't I?"

Meg became serious and looked about the staffroom nervously.

"If the sell-by is close, I can usually get them away between the booze shelves and the bargain bins - I just stick them in a corner behind something else in the store room - then leave that way - always make sure the car is parked close to the loading bay." She half whispered - half sang.

"Oh," Kimona was shocked, she had no idea, "right." A short silence followed.

"Look, remember you told me you used to be a professional photographer Kimona?"

"Wedding Photographer mostly," Kimona gently corrected her,

"Well, I was thinking that it would be nice to have the kids done - move on and all that - now they're getting older, you know?"

"Yah, absolutely," Kimona took another gulp. The last thing she wanted to do now - at this stage of her life - was to take more bloody mondain, lifeless photos - and particularly of kids.

"I'd make it worth your while," Meg was whispering tunefully again, "you know, anything you need?"

"Vodka?" Asked Kimona enthusiastically and a bit too quickly.

Meg pulled a painful look.

"No sell-buy on spirits darling."

Kimona liked the 'darling' bit and wondered if she could ask for more than just retail goods - but decided to stick with the booze.

"Wine then, strong wine - any colour and boxes of it." Could be pushing my luck a bit here, she thought.

"Yes," replied Meg quickly, "Easy-peasy, the box gets damaged - with a carefully placed jar of pasta sauce - you can't sell it at full price. The bag inside is fine of course. Five bags do you?"

Kimona wasted no time with an answer.

"Yah, great - but you've got to share one with me - soon." Her gaze was insistent.

"You're on." Said Meg and stood to go about her skilful and obviously well exercised shoplifting sideline.

"Wait - Meg?" Kimona jumped up and caught Meg up, "Can you get me a couple of small things today?"

"Like what?"

"I need a cheap pair of sunglasses and some wire."

Meg rolled up her eyes, as if to count in her head for a moment.

"No probs, meet me by my car after you're shift - finishing at ten?"

Kimona nodded.

"It's the white Electric Mercedes - reg - MEG 69".

FOUR

'PEACE VALLEY APPOINTMENT WITH COUNCILLOR HELEN - 14:30 - PLEASE RESPOND TO THIS MESSAGE WITHIN 24 HOURS TO CONFIRM YOUR APPOINTMENT - BE SMART - STAY APART' -

Pay-day - love it!

After shopping for her essentials, Kimona starts working on the broken pieces of glass from the smashed bottle, using the cheap sunglasses and copper wire Meg had acquired for her yesterday. A couple of drinks has steadied her elastoplasted hands, so no further lacerations should occur once she starts to try and search for the most compatible and complete pieces of broken bottle. She turns them until they fit together like a damaged Jigsaw. Then using, first the concrete at the bottom of the steps outside, and finishing with a nail file, she finally ground down the fractured pieces so they fit, almost perfectly, into the cheap sunglasses frame, where she had easily popped out the plastic lenses from earlier. Further strength was applied by fixing two photographic Ultraviolet filters (which appear clear to the naked eye) on the front of the sunglasses frame using multiple copper wire strips soldered together as mini clamps.

At Peace Valley Helen, Kimona's councillor, asks her permission for a trainee to sit in on their session - Kimona agrees, 'I've got no secrets' she lied.
"So, how's it goin' girl?"
"You tryin' to be black Helen?"
"No." Helen responded a little embarrassed. "This is just the way I talk when I'm relaxed with someone, I'm fond of Kimona."
"I'm a fifty-two-year-old crippled, black, lesbian." Kimona directed her statement at the trainee, a very young man with over-sized glasses.
"I only need to become morbidly obese, deaf or blind and I've ticked all the boxes - right?" The trainee didn't react.
"You seem a little tense today Kimona, anything in particular bothering you?" Asked Helen while breaking eye contact to make a note.

"Yah, actually there is ..." Kimona contemplated blurting out the Alien situation, but in her head counted to seven - reach for heaven - instead. Something Kimona's mother had instilled into her when she was very young, and her temper was starting to become an issue. One - for the Sun, make a large circle with your arms. Two - go to the zoo, close your eyes and see the animals. Three - climb a tree, mime a climb with arms and legs. Four - paint the door, make a painting action, swapping hands halfway. Five - get ready to dive, adopt a knees-bent, hands together pose and bounce a little. Six - build with bricks, stack the imaginary bricks from the floor up. Seven - reach for heaven, stretch your arms and face up to the sky.

The councillors waited patiently.

"It's you Helen."

"OK, how have I annoyed you Kimona?"

"You're acting all weird, not like normal. Drop the act girl!" Helen said nothing, just gave a nod to the trainee who asked the next question with a hint of eastern European in his accent.

"What exactly happens when you haven't had a drink for a while Kimona?"

"Heart starts to beat fast - then the shakes - what's that?" Kimona points towards a sketch book on the table half hidden underneath Helen's handbag.

"This?" Helen pulls it out and hands it to Kimona, "I saved it from the rubbish bins years ago. It's been in my car for ages, since I moved to a new house. I thought Martha might use it for inspiration in the art class, some of the drawings in there are amazing. It belonged to a neighbour of mine."

"It's very cool," Kimona thumbed through the sketch book. "Can I have it Helen?"

"What will you do with it Kimona?"

"I'll take the sketches out and put them in frames – got loads of A4's left from my previous incarnation as a photographer - remember? I'll put them on my wall next to my running certificates - I really like them, look at this one, it's amazing!"

The trainee spoke up again.

"That's right you used to run competitively didn't you Kimona?"

"Fastest in the county - four years running," All smirked at the obvious pun.

"Ok Kimona," Helen said, "they should be on a wall where somebody can appreciate them, take it, it's yours."

Kimona thanked Helen with sincerity and all feelings of annoyance where extinguished. Helen smiled and turned to the trainee,

"Kimona is physically addicted to alcohol," she turned back to Kimona for both acknowledgment and permission to continue, Kimona gave consent with a nod.

"In order to function properly in society, she works in retail, she self-medicates. We have explored various rehabilitation programs over the years, none of which have suited Kimona's unique case." Helen turns her attention back to Kimona. "It's not a protocol we would encourage here at Peace Valley, but I could administer Thymine, B12 and Temazepam - here at the center - three times a day - for two weeks. Provided of course that you will abstain from any alcohol what-so-ever for that period. What do you think Kimona? Can you do it?"

"I could do it, but why would I not drink Helen? What's at the end of the alcoholic rainbow? Have you seen the state of the world these days - there's more discrimination and segregation now, than ever. Na! Thanks, and all, but the only way to live in this state, is in an inebriated one." Helen looks disappointed and reluctantly makes another note.

"How many wines or G and T's do you have at night after doing good all day?" Kimona's question goes unanswered.

"The decision, as always Kimona, has to come from you. When you are ready, we will support you, but you really must try to take steps towards that. Giving up, gives us nothing to work with, you know?"

"I know." Kimona was sincere. "Don't get me wrong Helen - I do appreciate what you try and do for me, particularly the grief counselling stuff, it helped me out a lot there for a while, but the Citalopram, Diazepam and those other replacements for the booze ..."
Helen interrupted with a clinical statement.
"Those medications were not prescribed as replacements for alcohol consumption, but were put in place to assist with the anxiety symptoms experienced whilst weaning off alcohol ..."

"Ok," Kimona butted back in, "but never-the-less, those meds would have turned me into an anorexic zombie with no libido that just watched repeats on T.V. all day long."

"But the damage to your body Kimona," Helen sounded like her Mother for a moment.

"Have you read the side effects of some of those drugs Helen? And we both know how damaging they can be to the liver, right?"
Helen raises her eyebrows at the trainee, who makes his own note.

"Ok Kimona, would you mind if I went over the details of the car crash for our friend here?" Helen motioned towards the emotionless trainee.

Kimona shrugs apathetically, but her heart rate rises.

"Thank you. Would you like to tell him, or shall I?" Kimona points to Helen and sits back in the chair in a fake attempt the look comfortable.

"You can put straight anything I get wrong Kimona. Ok? On the seventh of September, twenty, twenty, Kimona, who was forty-two at the time, was involved in a car collision, she lost control and hit a tree. The accident claimed the life of her mother, whom she was rushing to the Hospital at the time and resulted in Kimona almost losing her leg. Kimona was breathalysed at the hospital and was found to be more than three times over the legal limit. A verdict of death by drink driving was awarded by the court, with any sentence being a suspended one. This was due to Kimona having to live with the fact that she had caused the death of her only living relative, her mother, and deemed by the court to be punishment enough."

"The dog was killed too." Kimona broke the silence. "I sometimes sit and hold my hand to my chest - feeling for a heartbeat. Sometimes willing it to stop, so I can sleep without clenching my fists when I wake. I held my dog's chest and felt her heart stop at the side of the road after the crash."

"What was her name?" Asked the trainee with softness in his voice.

"Doesn't matter does it?" Kimona said with an energized aggression.

"No, don't suppose it does." Said the trainee with a new-found arrogance.

"What matters now is you Kimona," added Helen diplomatically.

"Yes, your right!" Exclaimed Kimona with an even higher level of energy. "What matters right now is me, and others like me, the forgotten tribe. It's time to set the record straight and stand up for what is right and eliminate all that is bad!"

FIVE

The bright morning had developed into a very hot day, must have been thirty degrees. Kimona, true to her word, spent the next hour choosing her favourite drawings from the sketch book and looking for some empty A4 frames, but she had been mistaken, there weren't any. She instead decided to replace her running certificates with the new artwork, making sure to keep the certificates safe by leaving them in the back of frames also. There was now a cluster of seven, three in the middle with two rows above and below. After admiring them for a while, Kimona turned on the T.V. to catch the weather report for later. Her mouth was dry, so she opted for pineapple juice on top of her 'Insane Vodca'.

The first time she had experienced the positive effect of high functioning Vodka drinking was at a wedding she was photographing one summer. The best man gave her a very large one 'to settle the nerves' he had said, thoughtfully. And it did, so it became a staple after that. Any slightly stressful or potentially anxious social situation saw Kimona fuelled by alcohol. She soon realized that the small hip-flask amount, stealth-fully tucked away in the pocket of one of the camera bags, wasn't enough to reach the desired 'chilled out' effect. The affect that helped her not give a shit what colour she was, the fact that she was a female photographer so therefore naturally inexperienced as far as most wedding guests were concerned, and she became convinced that her limp was less severe - the joints and muscles lubricated by the Vodka. She only got drunk once.
It was a bikers wedding and as soon as the formalities were over, some of the old boys were popping a couple of Tramadol into bottles of Jack Daniels, which they sipped on and past around for the rest of the night. Kimona met the sister of the bride, heavily leather clad, tight trousers and waistcoat with nothing underneath. Her very impressive cleavage and neck was tattooed with a symmetrical design which, as the evening progressed, became the main focus of Kimona's camera lens.
The disproportionate attention didn't go un-noticed by the brides' sister, so much so that Kimona abandoned the idea of driving home and instead stayed the night. The morning however was disastrous.

It soon became evident why Kimona had woken with a sense of great disappointment. The brother in law had joined the women at some point through the night and once awakened by Kimona's attempt to slide out of the four-poster bed, locate and put on her clothes, asked her to go and get the married couple some breakfast and lots of coffee. Kimona stayed silent until she reached the doorway. "Yes masa - right away sir!" She slammed the door as hard as it would allow and, on her way out of the Hotel pushed over the 'Wedding of ...' sign in the lobby. As she sat in her car on the brink of tears, Kimona decided, for the first time on a morning, that a quick couple of drinks, from the extra bottle stashed away in the boot of the car, would be the best thing before the three hour drive back home. She stopped twice for top ups.

The glasses look ridiculous - but they are solid and more importantly, they fit.
Kimona took another drink that she had to force past her throat. The News presenter on T.V. was of Alien origin. "See, I ain't no Stakki!" Kimona had lapsed into native Caribbean again, confirming she was no 'mad person'. Her heart rate soars, and her breathing is only calmed by pacing around the room, but she will not remove the glasses from her face - instead she turns the channels on the remote control.
BBC News - alright. Loose Women - two out of five, Alien. Heno Aur - alright. Traffic Cops - the bad guy was - bad. Ramsay's Kitchen Nightmares - alright, but he's still a bastard. The welsh stuff and the old repeats seemed to be fine which made Kimona wonder if this Alien thing was new. 'A new evolution revolution.' She thought.
Pineapple drink - finished - Keys and Health Card ready - door locked - Glucosade bottle - glasses on - let's go!

It only takes two streets for Kimona to conclude that approximately one in every five citizens is Alien. She continues to walk through the town, with a surprising amount of people not taking any notice of her oversized and frankly grotesque glasses. She fights with her hyperventilation by stopping in the doorway in one of many, closed down, shops and takes a good gulp of neat 'Insane Vodca' hidden inside a Glucosade bottle she both carries and squeezes like a stress ball as she goes.

"This has to be stopped," she repeats under her breath, it helps with the breathing, "they're everywhere and nobody knows it."
Kimona had planned the root before leaving her flat, around the centre of town in a great big circle.

She was now on her way back when she felt the compulsion to stop. Kimona was looking down at a homeless – Alien - in another closed shop doorway and for the first time she wasn't afraid. This one had a big beard which may have softened his appearance somewhat. He looked so helpless and frail and not at all - a risk. She fingered inside her trouser pocket for some change which she very slowly lowered to a sensible height to drop into the homeless guys upturned beret. Kimona froze for a moment, open mouthed, until she realized she was far too close to him and closed it abruptly, fascinated with the face before her. It was pale Caucasian, but with deep red lines around the large black lifeless eyes and which ran right down past the very small mouth. The skin was lumpy, as if acne scared, on most of the face apart from the large forehead which had lines but was smooth. The eyes were the worst - unreadable.

"You can see me, can't you?" He said, the small tight mouth hardly moving.

Kimona jumped back to her standing position.

"You can see what I have become - and what will become of you soon enough." The man reaches out at Kimona, clutching at her trousers.

"I was like you ..."

Kimona silences him with a powerful kick to the chest and whips off the glasses, unable to cope with the situation any longer she runs as fast as her leg will carry her, home.

She tries to control her breathing, the way she used to in competition during and after a race, by stretching her body upright on the back of the closed door and reaching her neck up to the ceiling.

"In through the nose - out through the mouth." As she felt the panic leave her body - the rage entered. "They're all mad!"

She pulled the African spear from the wall,

"Maen nhw i gyd yn wallgof!"(welsh)

She smashed the T.V. screen with it.

"Di wulla dem a stakki!"(caribbean)

Empty bottles, plates, DVD's, books all flew through the air until finally one of the posters on the wall stopped her in her tracks. 'What if you're right?' It read, depicting a small shoal of white fish swimming below a sky-blue water, with one solitary black fish in the middle swimming the other way.

Kimona takes another drink and replaces the spear back onto the wall, her shoes ploughing through the carnage cluttered floor on the way to the bathroom.

She digs out a, now vintage, girly magazine to distract herself from the morning's discoveries, rolls a cigarette and sits on the toilet. After taking a half-hearted look through the pages of many nude women, Kimona plucks up the courage, with the help of yet another drink, to put on the glasses once more. At first all was well. A fact that strengthened her theory that the 'invasion' was a recent event. She gleefully started to thank and congratulate the models out loud; their names being shown at the top of each set. Kimona's giggly school-girl comments stopped abruptly after turning to a page of the magazine about a third of the way through. Sexy Sandra from Scunthorpe had become ugly Alien bitch from god knows where. Kimona was disgusted and threw down the magazine on the floor where it opened to the back pages, full of adverts. One in particular caught her eye. It was advertising a DVD 'Sick and tired of all those pesky Aliens around the place - the Amazonians will save us all!' The picture was of a scantily clad black tribal woman slaying a body painted green Alien woman with the use of a spear and shield.

SIX

The next day is hot again, but this time with an ever-present stormcloud diluting the blue from the sky, no direct sun and very oppressive.

"There's a storm coming," Kimona says to herself as she finishes the application of what could only be described as war paint, to her face using the mirror in her bathroom. She moves to the living room where she arms herself with the spear and shield and puts on the glasses. The uniform is complete, an old two-piece cowgirl costume from years ago now looks like the bikini of a tribal warrior.

As she exists the flat, not locking the door after her this time, she almost literally runs into two large bailiffs, both of Alien origin and presumably heading for her place. Kimona wastes no time in backing up and furiously stabbing at them with her spear, puncturing both their abdomens with multiple two-inch stab wounds until they hit the ground writhing in pain. She runs across the road away from the shocked onlookers and down to the next street, the busiest one in town. Kimona keeps moving along fast as she systematically identifies and attacks any Alien she sees. The campaign lasts only a few minutes but leaves more than twenty injured and Kimona in a state of shear exhaustion. The crowd look at her. She is standing, blood splattered, at the end of the street, her chest heaving as she gasps for more air. Some humans are crying and holding each other, then some stand from their positions of helping the wounded and slowly begin to move towards her. Their shouts and curses muffled under the sound of her beating heart. She removes the glasses, tucking them into her waistband and flees along the street, the other way, back towards the relative safety of her flat. Meg is standing by the railings, blocking Kimona's entrance to safety.

"Hay ... nice get up girl" says Meg excitedly. She is all dolled up and clutches three bottles of good wine. "I've come around for drinks ... and maybe more?"

Kimona doesn't want to test the glasses on her, so she holds the suddenly confused looking Meg by the shoulders as the police sirens fade up from a distance.

"Run Meg ... Just run away," Kimona kisses Meg quickly and passionately leaving a small smudge of blood on the poor woman's cheek.

"Just go ... Now!"
Meg drops the bottles which smash at Kimona's bare feet and runs away in a typically girly fashion, screaming with arms flailing about.
The increased volume of the sirens helps Kimona to snap out of the opportunity missed hypnosis she was lost in; she descends the steps to the flat and closes the door muting out the sound.
She is still out of breath as she lays down the shield and spear and picks up her phone which has been charging on the coffee table and starts to record video.

"This is just the beginning - I know they will come for me now - but others need to know," Kimona pulls out the glasses from her waistband, "this is the only way to truly know - these glasses reveal the truth - I will be leaving them hear in my bathroom, under the sink - so break in and take them if you want to take up the fight. One day history will see us as the heroes we are - and build statues in our honour."
The sound of police sirens has now penetrated the flat__ they're close. Kimona walks calmly towards the bathroom, proudly warning the broken bottle glasses. She removes what little clothes she has on in preparation to be detained, Meg will most probably have pointed the police in this direction and looks at herself in the mirror.
A piercing scream resonates and echoes though the bathroom as Kimona sees her reflection through the glasses. Her Alien reflection. She loses her composure and stubbles backward, quickly knocking the glasses from her face and continuing to stumble out of the room and into the kitchen. Kimona hears a voice calling her name.

"Mamma?" she asks out loud in a girl-like tone.

"Kimona," there's knocking at the kitchen window from the back ally where the bins are kept. "Kimona, come out here." It's the old cow from upstairs, the old Alien cow, but she looks nice now, without the glasses on.

"Kimona, come with me. I'll keep you safe."
Dazed and confused Kimona opens the back door to the ally, where the neighbour suddenly grabs hold of her with a strong grip and guides her weakened, naked body up the steps of the fire escape and into her own flat a story above.
The old woman promptly wraps Kimona in a long dressing gown, puts an afro wig on her head and saturates a pink flannel with running hot water from the kitchen sink.

She wipes Kimona's blood and war-paint streaked face hard with the flannel until a crashing sound of the police entering Kimona's flat below makes them both jump, inspiring the old woman to further drag Kimona into the living room where she sat the younger, and much smaller, woman on her lap, pulling Kimona into her bosom and holding her there, tight while they both rocked subtlety, back and forth, in the large wooden chair.

"I will look after you," the old woman said as her hand gently cupped Kimona's ear. It was an attempt to stifle the shouts of 'armed police' and sounds of destruction from the flat below.

"I used to be a Nurse you know,"

"They're gonna find me." Kimona said with a large twitch from the hip.

"They won't - you know they all think we look the same don't you. You just stay right there. It'll be just fine - you see."
Kimona rubbed her head into the old woman's plumpness like a contented cat, thoughts of her own mother flooding her mind.

"You can stay here - with me," said the old woman softly. "We'll get rid of those nasty habits of yours - and when I die - this place will belong to you."
Kimona didn't react, she was far too comfortable.

"Yes, I own this flat - bought it some years ago now," the old woman rocked the chair a little more vigorously as she heard the police knocking on neighbours' doors, "I had to sell my house you see - to pay for legal costs. My boy was murdered by three rich white boys on a summers' night long ago. All three of them boys - sons of bitches - and an estate agent - a council manager and a magistrate would you believe.

I lost the case and even had to pay those white boys damages - de-fer-mation of - character they said."
The old woman glanced at the flat door along the short corridor from where she sat as she heard the heavy boots ascending the staircase.
"You know what those boys did? After they took my boy away from me? And after they took what was left of me in court that day? They smirked at me - god knows, those boys smirked at me."
The boots stopped.

"Now you just hush now there girl, let me do the talking."
The door is knocked, briskly three times.

"Come on in - it's open!" The old woman straightens the wig on Kimona's head, then tightens her grip on her even further, as she shouts just loud enough. The police enter through the doorway - three then five men all pointing their guns in different directions, the green laser beams from the end of each, cutting into the dusty air. The man in front looks dead ahead.

"Have you seen the woman from the flat below Ma'am?"

"No sir, just me and my daughter here," Kimona wriggles a bit with a whimper, "she's very anxious, we're shielders" mouths the old woman almost inaudibly. The policeman at the front pauses for a moment looks from the old woman to a curled up Kimona and back again. A distant rumble of thunder breaks the tense silence.

"All clear here!" bellows the policeman at the front, the message is reverberated down the line as the group slowly exit the exact way they entered, just in reverse. Just before the policeman in front reached the door, backwards, he gave a little wink to the old woman, who gave a little wink back. A loud crack of thunder disturbed Kimona again as the door was closed. She looked up at the old neighbour and smiled as the heavens opened outside.

END

ALL THIS TIME

V.O.O.D.O.O.
MURDER OF CROWS (PART II)

V.O.O.D.O.O.:
MURDER OF CROWS
PART II

VII

SATURDAY 31 OCT

19 grenades and ten guns. I was accumulating various weaponry ready to take with us to my safe-house at Clover Sands, when Othello turned up at the back door of the flat. Callahan was waiting for me at his place, his wife now safely re-located.

'It's a bit early for that Othello.' I told him as I stood in the kitchen. He looked friendly as he showed me a very strange looking bottle of something. 'I've got some things to do, maybe later, yes?'
I had successfully packed the last weapon into a large hold-all just as he had let himself in.

'Oh, come on Victor, what ever happened to the what the hell, like in the summer? Comfortably numb for weeks on end.' I deduced that Othello had already had one or two this morning, which was interesting. Where had he had them? If he'd taken a morning drink at home, he would've had to drive ten miles into Michael's Town.
No, he'd already had a drink with someone else before coming here — Dutch courage maybe?

I tuned back into what he was saying.
'And anyway, we're in lockdown again. What can there be to do that's so urgent?'
I looked at the bottle then back at him, wondering how much he knew and what the true ingredients of that liquid inside were.

'I know what you're thinking Victor - but you're wrong.' said Othello. 'I know you've been suspended, hell, that's why I'm here. To lend my support. Delilah was going to come as well but she's got to get her sprog through her homework on time, so couldn't make it. Look you can choose the glasses and I'll even have the first drink myself - and you can pour it.'

'Grab a seat Othello.' I threw him a smile as I reached out beside him and closed the door. 'I'll get some glasses.' I looked at two identical coffee cups - both black - and after checking Othello positioning himself by the small kitchen table, I carefully but swiftly put one onto the floor, obscured by my feet. I then grabbed myself a chair, with the second cup in hand, and made sure one of the front legs found its way into the first cup, quickly sliding it towards and just underneath the table edge. I gave Othello a third coffee cup from the draining board.

'Only things that are clean I'm afraid Othello.' He didn't seem to mind as he offered me the bottle to open. I let him pour. I pretend to drink while Othello put the cup to his lips. His hand was steady, but he had said very little so far, so I instigated conversation.

'I'll just have the one for now Othello, if that's alright with you. I want to tidy up the workshop - get rid of some bad wood.'
He stated he also had some clearing up to do, so that was fine.

The air had become tense, both of us trying to read the thoughts, or intention - if any - I still wasn't sure - of the other.

'Weird looking bottle Othello - you make it?' I started to roll a cigarette from the paraphernalia on the table. Othello chose one of his own manufactured, multi-coloured cocktail versions as he answered.

'No, I got it from that grotty pub we went to last Christmas. The brewery was selling off all the stuff.'

'Yes, I heard.' I glanced at the, semi-visible, crow sculpture in the next room then knocked my lighter from the table, making it look accidental, but quickly picking it up whilst moving the chair accordingly and switching the cups.

'Yah, stunning isn't it?' I'd got away with it. Othello was examining the bottle.

'Hand blown you know and signed at the bottom by someone called Gethin. Unknown to me, but the craftsmanship is superb, don't you think Victor?'

I took the bottle from him and agreed. I suddenly felt sorry for my drinking buddy. Something was up, he hadn't mentioned my suspension details or Odette yet. I mimed the finishing of the drink by throwing the cup vertically with a little slurp for good measure. Once the empty cup was back on the table I looked at Othello and got the sense that he was torn between them and me, that was until he spoke again, this time back to his normal speed and vitality and with a tone of professionalism. As if the deal was done and now it's time to go home. I dropped my eyelids and over-blinked a few times while slowly moving my head from side to side.

'Woo ... Strong stuff that Othello.' I slightly slurred his name for added effect and dropped my body into a semi-collapsed state in the chair.

'Yes ... Well I'll be leaving you now Victor. Have a little lie down my friend.'
He looked a little sad, but I was beyond that now. Othello left the way he came, via the fire escape at the back of the building, leaving me slumped at the kitchen table.
We met again soon after - very soon after - at the end of the ally-way that comes out at the promenade side of the building.
I struck an out of breath silhouette holding the strange looking bottle at my side and Othello, failed to hold his jaw shut.

'How d'you do it Othello?' I slowly walked towards him, he had nowhere to go. 'I'm guessing you took an antidote before you arrived - am I right?'

'Victor - how the hell?' The proverbial penny dropped. 'You didn't drink it did you.' He looked disappointed in himself which really pissed me off. I grabbed hold of the skinny man and pushed him back down the ally and hard against the cool stone wall.

'Would it have killed me Othello?' My spittle forcing him to rapidly blink.

'I just do am I'm told Victor, just like you. Please don't hurt me.'

'I need to know if Odette wants me dead - so talk or it'll be a very long time before you're able to hold a wine-glass again.' I swiftly jerk his arm behind his own back, holding it tight by the wrist. He knows I can and will break it. A very lenient punishment by my standards.

'Ok ... Ok... my orders were to calm you down for a while, a little siesta - that's all. It would've put you to sleep for a couple of days - that's all - help you to chill for a bit. We'd be doing you a favour really, helping you out.'

'Ok Othello ... so if I took you and this bottle round to Delilah's place - she'd only get tired and sleep for a while - right?' Again, he knew I would if I had to.

'I ... I ...'

'Your hesitation tells me everything I need to know Othello.' I slam him against the wall again. 'I should kill you where you stand.' Othello nods in agreement as he sobs. 'But I won't.' This time shaking his head in agreement. 'I want you to go back to Odette - with a warning. Play with hungry dogs and you'll get bitten.' Something I heard translated to me in Sierra Leone years ago. 'You tell her that.' Othello agreed as I let my grip loosen.

'Get in the van and I'll drop you off ...' I stopped myself saying, at her place. Othello could tell Odette remotely from his place. A sudden 'No' prompted me to tighten up again.

'No?' I asked. 'Why not Othello? - Othello!'

'Orien's been to it!' His answer was immediate.

'It's loaded with explosives is it? - Bloody hell you lot have wasted no time; I'll give you that. Odette's coming at me with all guns blazing then?' Othello confirmed it. I let my grip go once more, then to my astonishment he asked me for the bottle back.

'No, you bloody-well can't have it. I'm going to wash it out and chuck it in the bin. Now bugger-off and deliver that message to Odette.'

'Ok Victor - don't stress.' His elated confidence retuned with the realization his life would be spared.

'Do it straight away Othello - that's a warning.'

I returned to the flat, which would be relatively safe now. Voodoo would assume I'd go to ground elsewhere after Othello's failed visit.

With the van out of service I was forced to contact Callahan and tell him to make his own way here, to the flat, as soon as he could. In the meantime, I ordered some flowers from the local florist, Delilah, using another name and accent of course.

I had deliberately chosen a delivery address close to Delilah's home hoping she would leave the child behind and, as I watched her approach that night from my unlit hiding place, was relieved that she had. I infiltrated her before she reached the irrelevant address. She was shocked to see me but soon settled back into her demure persona.

'Delilah - you have to talk to Odette for me. Two of us will have much more clout - she's playing a very dangerous and unnecessarily stupid game.'

'I will talk to Odette Victor. Will you come in if I ok it?'

The comment was a classic entrapment manoeuvre, unworthy, or so I thought, of Delilah's intellect. I told her - no.

'Would you have killed Othello this morning Victor?'

'He was sent to poison me Delilah. What would you have done?' The conversation had become pointless. I gave her my business card with the phone number that Odette already had and watched her walk away.

Any feelings of past intimacy or comradeship faded away, along with the image of her and her flowers slowly disappearing out of the light and into the darkness of the night. It was time to put these new feelings aside and up my own game.

VIII

SUNDAY 1 NOV

Callahan eventually completed his theoretical work and together with my help, we sent a package to a colleague of his in Brussels for further analysis. When I returned from the post office, I found that Callahan had begun to celebrate the possible breakthrough with my scotch. I snatched it away from the doctor and replaced it with the address of the safe-house together with instructions for the trip through the Screaming Mountains and an order to leave immediately. He agreed without dispute and assumed he would need the keys to my van.

'You haven't got a car, have you?' I asked, already knowing the answer.

'I came by taxi.' Callahan said. I had neglected to warn him not to.

'I'll get you one.'
Omar had previously supplied me with software that changed car ownership details, to be used in conjunction with false plates stored at the Market Hall. The software would change dates and details of any car on the national register source based in Swansea, on the mainland. He had also supplied a skeleton key which would only work with Peugeots, 2012 plate or earlier, still very common around the town.

'I can use my wife's car.' Callahan interjected. I abruptly reminded him that was a very shit idea.

'Not that one, she's got another, an old classic, in a lock-up, in town.' He continued to tell me its whereabouts which was within walking distance and stressed he would be happier driving that. It would save me the bother of finding an applicable Peugeot, so I escorted him and gave some further instructions before I saw him off. It was pissing down by now so I tried the car radio for the weather report, but the bloody thing wouldn't work properly. Lastly, I gave Callahan a burner phone.

'Contact me when you get there and then turn the phone off. Turn it on again every day at 12:00 - until - 14:00. Don't forget. However, you can contact me, my number is the only one on there, using only this phone at any time. If anybody else answers - don't trust them - they would've just killed me.'

It was 13:50 and still no answer on Callahan's burner phone after the seventh attempt. He should have arrived at my safe-house about an hour before. I had got the distinct impression that the doctor was more than capable of following the instructions given, unlike many of his contemporaries. I find that academics, while most are more than competent within their prospective fields, can lack the aptitude to be affective when following simple everyday tasks that they're not used to. I decided to activate the high-tech doorbell, another piece of tech previously supplied to me by Omar when I set up my safe-house. It's accessed via my laptop. As well as a hidden camera, including audio, it has a built-in visitor log. It's activated by the front door opening rather than motion detection, as it picks up every fox, hare and badger in the area otherwise.
There was and had been - nothing. Callahan had never reached my safe-house.

As a storm-filled evening sky descended I got a hankering for freshly baked bread and my feet got itchy. I needed to know if the wife's car had been rigged, so I decided to pay Orien the Baker - come explosive and incendiary devices expert - a visit.

It started raining - heavily, it didn't last long but soaked me through. Orien lived in town, Heart & Soul Road to be precise. I'd been to a party at his place a couple of years ago, little booze but a hell of a lot of drugs going on. Not really my sort of thing.
I eyed-up the place for some time. Orien lived on the ground floor of an old Georgian style Terrace house, very common in the town. The wheelie bins outside, behind the Victorian style railings and at the side of an overgrown path, had the number of the house - sixty-six. One big bin and another two smaller next to it gave the impression that the devil might reside inside.
I easily spotted three bodies through the dust-coloured, ripped up, net curtains at the large front window. Orien lived with, god knows how many, like-minded friends. I needed to talk with him privately. I couldn't phone first as it might spark a counter-attack. Orien was a massive pothead but could be as sharp as a pin when needed to be. I assumed at this point, and as a result of Othello's visit, that Odette had ordered some, or maybe all, the members of voodoo to organize my demise. So, an impromptu friendly visit should catch him off-guard. It seemed the most sensible and non-violent option. The bomb-maker-baker had always proclaimed that he was a pacifist at heart.
My senses, already acute as a matter a habit, were first aroused when Orien shot up from his grungy armchair before I fully reached the front door.

Obviously, some sort of early warning signal. An invisible broken laser or something similar, supplied by Omar no doubt. So, as soon as I had rang the doorbell I stood to the side and waited. My eyes darting all over the frontage of the building anticipating an attack from above. I thought of those large pales of boiling hot tar they used to throw over the castle walls, incapacitating, to say the least, the invading army below. The front door latch clicked, and it opened gently. I was greeted by Othello, again clutching a bottle of something.

'Hello ... Victor.' He said loudly, a little pissed or stoned by the sound of it.

'You're not offering me one this time Othello?' I gestured towards the bottle with my head whilst my eyes peered either side of his and down the long, narrow, dimly lit corridor behind him.

'No - silly.' He said giving a limp slap to my upper arm. 'I'm on my way-out Victor.' Othello had to push his way past me through the doorway, where once outside, shouted back into the corridor.

'Orien ... Victor's here to see you!' That was the point at which I reached out and grabbed hold of Othello's thin jacket with a tight clenched fist, stunting his quickened exit.

'Victor, let go of me!' Again, loud enough to be heard inside the house. I looked back down the corridor just in time to see Orien appear from a side door - a friend appeared behind him holding a cardboard box at waist level. Orien was holding something small and colourful in his hand, which he twisted once and threw towards me with speed and accuracy.

It stuck to my wet jacket - like a kid's toy - it had little red suckers extruding from a purple sphere, each one a small arm with an open palmed hand. Strangely it had more than a passing resemblance to a microscopic image of the virus. I knew I had very little time and as Othello had suddenly darted towards the side of the door frame, painfully jolting my elbow joint in the process, I let go of him and instantly whipped off my jacket, half throwing, half kicking it underneath the large window at the front of the house. The sticky mini-grenade made a pop and hissed from one end - it looked like a shaken bottle of beer being opened - then the big bang. Hot shrapnel flying outwards at every angle. It was quite localized but nasty. Many of the pieces embedded themselves into the half-rotten woodwork surrounding the window, releasing an acrid line of smoke. Over my protective forearm, which was now across my face, I rushed towards Orien and his lacky with the cardboard box at the entrance to the house. Orien threw another as soon as he saw me, I twisted, it missed and landed, instantly sticking without rolling, onto the path behind me. Another came my way - and another. Somehow, I managed to avoid them. If one had got stuck on me, I'd be fucked - I couldn't pull it off as it would stick to my hand. How the hell was I going to get anywhere near this guy and put him out of action without one of his sticky toys blowing a chunk out of me in the process? Othello was shouting at Orien.

'Let me out Orien - for god's sake!'

I decided to slide to the side of door frame, knocking Othello into next doors' hedge, there wasn't room for two. The first mini grenades were exploding on the path, showering us with stone chippings and old cement.

I grabbed Othello from his uncomfortable position embedded in the hedge, he thanked me and looked sincere. That was until I spun him around and held him, this time with both clenched fists, in front of the open doorway. He was instantly pelted with three sticky grenades. The bombardment stopped as Orien realized that, he'd got the wrong man. Othello let out a painfully high-pitched scream as I got behind him, pulled my Beretta from its shoulder holster, sent a couple of inaccurate shots towards Orien and gave Othello an unfortunately weak push into the corridor. This was mainly due to the pain in my elbow. Othello was able to stay upright and dance his way back past me to the outside again. I quickly moved for cover at the window side once more as Othello ran like a man on fire down the path. Inexplicably he then threw himself into the larger of the three wheelie bins standing at the end of the garden. The lid closed after him just in time to hear the three dull pops - then one large bang. The smoke cleared very quickly. The large bin now resembled a well-used Christmas candle. Blades of green wax leaning away from the flame and a liquid red puddle at the centre. I took no time at beating the half-rotten wooden windowsill from the wall using the base of my fist. I held it out in front of me as I stood, side on, in the doorway once more.
I was lucky. One stuck to the wood so I threw it back in. I saw it slide all the way to Orien's feet as I reached in and closed the front door with such an almighty slam,
I thought the grenade had gone off prematurely. It did a few seconds later. By which point I was standing in front of the large window again pointing and trailing my pistol sight through the holes in the net curtains towards the three bodies scurrying back into the room from the corridor.

Orien dived into the cardboard box thrown onto the large sofa by his hysterical friend. He held a sticky mini grenade above his head, looking straight at me and ready to throw. We were both in check. If he throws the grenade in my direction, it will attach itself to the window and explode in the room. And if I break the window to get an accurate shot at Orien, he would also have a clear line of sight on me. We stared at each other our minds desperately trying to be the first to come up with the checkmate move. In my experience you must sometimes just go with the first idea that enters your head and hope for the best. I suddenly broke eye contact with Orien, double checking where the cardboard box was located, then pulled the trigger on the Beretta. I tried my best to only blink once as the glass shattered inwards and outwards. My eyes were open when Orien threw the sticky grenade. I never played Cricket, but I was very good at Rounders at primary school, all I had to do was adopt a sort of reverse batting technique - it worked. The grenade stuck solidly to the side of the Beretta enabling me to then throw the pistol towards the cardboard box, open on the sofa. Amazingly it landed right inside. The three flat mates hardly had time to verbally react before the pop hissed. I threw myself to the ground at the foot of the closed front door. The explosion was huge. I had protected my ears with forefingers.
So only once removed could I hear the light material and odd body part hit the wet ground outside the window in the immediate aftermath. As I stood up and dusted myself down, I thought of Othello and the time we had spent together over the summer. Despite my recent conversion to sentimentality, I felt very little. How can anyone say rest in peace? When you know the poor bastard is now in pieces.

MONDAY 2 NOV

It was the early hours of the next day when the Fire engines and Police cars past me on my way back to the flat. I'd never called it home, or mine. I'd never called anywhere home, ever.

I unlocked the door, first the lock at handle height, then the deadlocking night latch at the top.
Someone was in there. I have a little trick with an elastic band. Every time I leave the flat, I fit the rubber-band around the moving part of the night latch. Once I return, I can just about see the thing hit the floor, as it is so light. It was already grounded when I opened the door. Easy to miss for an intruder not looking for it, nothing unusual about a stray elastic band on the floor if they noticed it. I was cold, wet, exhausted and my bloody elbow was killing me. I contemplated closing the door and buggering off, to join Callahan, at my safe-house instead.
Omar, Delilah and Odette were the only voodoo members left.
I assumed it would be the last field agent with any real experience of combat - that was Omar.
I smelt my way into the flat, you can smell some types of plastic explosive at close quarters. I couldn't - but someone was there. Maybe Delilah with a message or Odette herself willing to call a cease-fire and strike a deal. Stop the level of carnage that even she presumably couldn't have known the full extent of yet.

'Come on then voodoo ...' I didn't need to shout as it was so late and didn't want to rouse any of the other tenants. 'I'm tired and have an injured arm. Do we really have to do this right now?'

I didn't worry that my would-be assailant, which ever one that might be, would be suddenly alerted of my presence as they should have known I was already there. The tired and injured information was true but also a diversion technique, making them believe they already have some sort of an advantage over me. I've been playing that game since primary school. The resident tough nuts – three usually – would test any new boy to see if he was fit to be one of them – by following him around the yard at break-time, taunting and eventually cornering him. Well I would choose the corner and when the time was right, when they started to bounce with the excitement of imminent violence, I'd pounce. The beating they got was of on a level they didn't understand or had ever experienced before. You could see it on their puppy-fat faces, the first realization of mortality – 'Please stop.' I only had to do it once, they'd all follow me then as my reputation would exceed me. That is until I had to move to the next school and start all over again.

All voodoo members were aware that I was the deadliest at close quarter combat. I took a long intake of air which filled my lungs and expanded my chest as I found the most painful part of my elbow with my other hand and squeezed, tight. The air rushed back out of my body from behind exposed, clenched teeth. The adrenaline surged as I cricked my neck one way and the other – I was ready – so I slammed the door behind me, with a fuck it attitude. The flat was dark and still with only my own breathlessness induced by the self-inflicted elbow pain audible, so I stopped it by holding it. I looked around willing my eyes to adjust to the darkness faster than they were. I was looking for two things. One, trip wires or some other kind of booby-trap at my feet or neck height.

The other, a seductress lounged on the sofa, or an old Quartermaster sitting at my kitchen table. As I reached the crow sculpture, it's silhouette now dominating the space in front of the main window, all areas were checked and clear. Then, as I had to inhale, I saw a minuscule movement from the corner of my eye lurking in the short alcove before the closed doorway to the bathroom about eight feet away.

'I am unarmed ...' I raised my arms slowly as I faced the blacked-out alcove. 'You're welcome to check for weapons if you wish.'
I walked, one slow step at a time, until my foe was recognizable. It was Omar. He was wearing a pair of old night vision goggles. The sort that had long and heavy lenses, one longer than the other sticking outwards a good eight inches and weighing on his classical Arabian nose. He was holding a small silenced pistol, pointing it at me from his hip.

'Bit low-tech for you Omar?' My comment forcing the smallest of smiles just visible on his semi-lit lips.

'Sorry Victor.' He said.
That was the cue - no time left for pleasantries or diplomacy - that's the universal trigger word - 'sorry.'. All I had to hand was the crow sculpture. I flew behind it simultaneously pulling it in front of me. It worked. The small .22 bullet ricocheted off its surface producing a bright light-orange spark. I knew another would follow in less than a second, Omar might have been wearing twenty-year-old night vision goggles, but the pistol was a new Glock. My next move was purely a reflex. The heavy sculpture seemed to push halfway into Omar's body almost becoming enveloped like a hot-dog in a finger roll.

My arms were at full length as I continued to push as hard as I could, pinning Omar between the sculpture and the closed bathroom door behind him. A brief stream of vomit spayed from either side of the sculpture - his body spasmed and I heard the Glock drop to the floor - he was hurt. I had heard a puzzling sound on impact but had put it down to air escaping from whatever orifice of the body - you'd be surprised what sounds you can hear when a body takes an almighty whack - but I wasn't prepared for the source of the sound. I peeled the sculpture away from Omar's, now limp, body and saw that the long night vision lenses were level to where his eyes should have been. He slid down to a sleeping drunk position on the floor. There was no blood, apart from a large gash on the bridge of his broken nose, and no life. Just those haunting green tinted lenses staring uninterruptedly back at me.

    I opened the curtains, hoping the morning light would revitalize my mind. The promenade was deserted. It wasn't raining but judging by the large puddles reflecting the pastel, multi-coloured houses of the half-a-mile long prom terrace, it had been through the night. I always slept lightly so normally rainfall would be enough of an interruption to remember the next day. I must have slept like a top my well-worn stiff neck being testament of that. I contemplated breakfast but the faint hint of vomit and excrement emanating from Omar's covered up corpse put me off and also prevented my clean entry into the bathroom.
The plan was to visit Odette at her fish-bowl house, halfway up South Hill. I got dressed and slithered Omar's pistol away from his scarecrow-like legs, checked the magazine and chamber then tucked it into the back of my trousers, under my raincoat. There were plenty of weapons still in the hold-all in the kitchen,

but most were assault rifles, not required for this visit, besides I already had my blade with me. An assassin always starts his or her career with a long-range weapon, such as a sniper rifle which happens to be large in size. A proficient assassin ends up using a very close up weapon like a knife, which is small.
I suddenly thought of the van still parked outside and loaded with explosives. Orien would normally have de-activated an unused car-bomb but of course he was currently indisposed, or should I say in-de-garden. Some poor bastard of a garage recovery driver would eventually get blown to bits, along with god knows who else on the street. I quickly decided and prepared a note to place onto the windscreen on my way to Odette's place, in case I didn't make it back.

IX

Access to Odette's house was very quick and a lot easier than I had anticipated. Luckily the legless Pekingese was taking a shit in the garden at the back of the house, so I broke my cover from within the evergreens and simply let myself in through the back door which was ajar.
Odette was chopping a very freshly slaughtered chicken into portions when she turned and acknowledged my presence in her kitchen. She carried on with her task regardless, throwing the head and feet from the carcass into a large white bucket beside her on the floor. Small black and white feathers were sent into the air as the body parts landed softly and silently. Once finished Odette called the dog by name as she washed and dried her hands. The Pekingese came waddling in obediently and she gave me a small nod of appreciation for the fact he was still alive. Truth is, if he were a guard dog of any kind, he would be dead by now.

'White or red Victor?' Odette held two empty wine glasses of different sizes.

'A bit early for me I think Odette.'

'Rubbish! I always partake in a small libation whilst preparing the evening meal, whatever the time of day. Red!' She filled and passed me a large glass of red wine.

'Red - with chicken?'

'It's Coq au Vin smart-arse. Now let's sit, in there.'
We moved to the sitting room. I very politely, as well as tactically, let her enter and sit first. I talked about Callahan and the very real possibility of a vaccine being produced in record time.

Odette wasn't surprised or interested, instead she specified that this was not the right time for a vaccine. It made no sense to me, so I demanded to know why.

    'Ok Victor ... It's the bames.'

    'The what?' I was at a loss.

    'B.A.M.E. The acronym stands for Black, Asian and Minority Ethnic and is defined as all ethnic groups except White ethnic groups.'

    'What about it?'

    'This country, as well as many of her allies will be in a state of economic ruin unless something decisive is previsioned for - now.'

    'Like what?' I spoke cautiously as I thought I knew where this was going.

    'Oh, for god's sake Victor. The bame community, together with the vulnerable and the morbidly obese, are the most at risk of dying from this thing. That's exactly what needs to happen before the rest of society is vaccinated.'

    'My god. That's millions of people across the continent!'

    'A very small percentage of the over-all population of this country, I think you'll find. But the necessary amount to give us the chance of recovering from an economic nightmare that will last the duration of a generation.'

    'That's barbaric. What the hell gives this government the right to decide who lives and dies?'

    'Who's talking about the government Victor?'

    'What do you mean? Our bosses at Whitehall Odette.'

    'We don't have any Victor. We haven't since 2010. I run this outfit now and have done, successfully, for the last ten years. My father invested well and with a bit of luck and a hell of a lot of British pluck, he earned a fortune, all of which is now entrusted to me.'

    'Ten years rouge?'

'I've been paying your wages, bonuses and expenses since Cameron and Clegg cut our budget and reduced us to glorified internet watchers, answerable directly to G.C.H.Q. Omar keeps them happy enough to stay off my back so I can concentrate on the more pressing matters that are affecting this country's growth, reputation and standing in the world.'

My god I thought. She's gone insane, lost the bloody plot. All those missions I carried out on behalf of the crown. Who do I get in touch with? Who do I ask for at the Home Office? They deny our very existence. Victor is an unknown name, reporting to be part of V.O.O.D.O.O. which is a non-existent organization.

'So, what about when the virus is left to its own devises Odette? To circulate and mutate over and over again. It poses more risk to your fit, slim, young and white population then, doesn't it?'

'Victor ... Victor ... You've been watching the news again haven't you.'

'You patronizing bitch! You don't even know ... Even you ... With all your years of experience. You don't have the answers Odette!' I had an unfortunate lump in my throat and quiver to my voice, so I kept my words short.

'Actually, I think you'll find I do Victor. And if you give it enough thought, you'll also be in agreement.'
She smiled the sort of smile that disappeared as fast as it appeared. A patronizing and victorious expression.

'So what the hell have we all being doing for the last ten years? What's it all been for?'

'I told you Victor ... This country. All you and your colleagues have done has been in the interest of Great Britain. You just have to trust me on that.'

I searched my brain for the most recent missions I had been involved with and knew something about.

'Wildfires in Oz - thirty-four dead.' I said, more like an answer than a question. Odette spent no time in answering.

'Orien's incendiaries were designed as a distraction and hopeful elimination of Australian S.A.S. prosecution witnesses that lived at the epicentre and were due to testify. Didn't work as well as I'd hoped I'm afraid. The report, due out at the end of this year will probably now find that Australian special forces unlawfully killed thirty-nine people in Afghanistan between 2005 and 2016. Can't win em' all Victor'

'What about Omar and Delilah's trip to Tehran? That Ukrainian 737 crash.'

'Yes ... There was an Irani scientist, his name escapes me, on board who had a theory about the new virus. Very much like your Doctor Callahan scenario. Iran took the blame with a promise from us to be the first middle eastern country to receive an effective vaccine, once available of course.'

'Who do these foreign governments think they're dealing with when you cut these deals Odette?'

'Who cares! They don't. As long as the deal suits them, they'll participate.
And as you know Victor, once I get started, I can be very persuasive.'

'Is that what you've been up to on your trips to the states? Rallying up support for your one-woman global domination scheme?'

'In a way yes. You helped too remember, the Beirut port?'

'I'd rather forget.'

'Both the U.S. political parties are important Victor, whether we like it or not. Twenty years ago they were funding the I.R.A.

now they are quite happy to fund any organization that can assure an efficient result whilst keeping their name out of it as it were. Your massive oil spill into the Ambarnaya river helped with that Victor. Othello helped the South Koreans, putting Kim Il-sung out of action for a while. My American friends were worried he might take advantage of the wests weakened state.
However, I gained the trust of the Democrats, with some help from Omar. He found a teenager from Florida who took over the twitter account of Mr. Biden, amongst others, we handed him over. They were very grateful, so I offered more help. Particularly with the up and coming election results.'

    'And Wuhan?' I hesitantly asked.

    'Ahh, that was another liaison with our American friends. China's economy was becoming far too successful. It was meant to be contained there, like the SARRS, but the textiles factory you left the package at had hundreds of Chinese workers about to depart for Italy. They use them a lot apparently, illegally of course. They're a huge part of the fashion industry in the larger Italian Cities. We didn't know that.'
There began a moment of silence. I shook my head as I continued the conversation.

    'All you do is condemn the people of this world to misery.'

    'Hah, and since when have you cared about the people of the world Victor?' Odette sounded like she should have finished her sentence with a snarl.

    'Whatever happened to protecting democracy, the great western way of life. I used to be proud - disposing of the bad guys - when we knew who and where they were that is.'

    '9/11 changed all that Victor. Oil and gold have always been important but national economy is the new king -

the governments are run by accountants. They say, it would be nice if we could get a contract for this or build a factory for that, especially if the factory is planned to be built in a marginal constituency - something else that doesn't seem to exist anymore. If a bridge collapses in a South American country, who gets the steel contract? Sheffield, Llanelli or China? That will depend on who collapsed the bridge in the first place. It's all about business - just business Victor. You mustn't take it so personally.'
I took another sip of wine and calmed myself down once I saw my hand quiver in super close-up. We sat silently once more. I watched Odette pour herself another half-glass with the steadiest of hands.
I leant towards her and gently touched the side of her head. She sat perfectly relaxed as I continued downwards reaching the side of her face and further to her neck.
The venous blood ran through the top of her flowery blouse almost staining it black. She noticed it creeping towards her chest before she felt the mortal incision, made by the tiny blade tucked between my fingers, to her jugular vein.

    'What is this?' She asked looking down at her left breast.

    'It's not personal Odette - just business.' I replied softly.

Odette let out a gentle sigh as if relieved in a way and then closed her eyes. The glass followed the spilt wine to the floor. The only indication of unconsciousness which will imminently lead to death. The Pekingese turned up and started licking the red wine from the mushy puddle on the carpet. It stopped and looked up towards the large glass wall that had the best view of the town I'd ever seen. While still sat I followed its eyes with mine.

Suddenly the quiet tranquillity was broken by the popping of bullets hitting and embedding themselves in the wall behind me. The shattering of glass came after - high velocity bullets are faster than falling glass.
I instantly went to ground and positioned myself in between the armchairs one of which still housed Odette, her body now disrespectfully bullet wounded. The ceiling-to-floor glass wall was very helpful in aiding my view of the would-be assailant - it was Delilah. She made no attempt to take any natural cover. Just stood in the middle of the path leading to the house with an M4 Carbine, complete with M203 Grenade Launcher, which looked far too large for her slender fingers and thin arms to cope with - explained why she was shooting from the hip, like Scar-face. Her long fingered, perfectly manicured, hand was incorrectly holding the thirty-round magazine for support as she continued to pepper bullets into the sitting room, but they would soon run out. She looked upset. Even from my hundred-meter distance, I could see that her eye make-up had run onto her cheeks.
I couldn't help thinking of her daughter - they only had each other - but I couldn't be stopped, not now and definitely not like this.
I prepped Omar's Glock - locked and loaded. Delilah had run out of bullets - so I flew through the now glassless wall, adopted a slightly squatted stance and pointed my weapon - held in a classic Cup n' Saucer target shooting hold - at the woman I once could've loved.

'Delilah!' I shouted, hoping to stop her in her tracks. She was fumbling, reaching into her handbag for another long magazine. I could safely assume there was no grenade loaded in the launcher - thank fuck. However, if she loads the next magazine - I'm dead anyway.

'One chance girl - we'll talk - put it down Delilah. Please!'
She said nothing - didn't even look at me. Just whimpered a little as she got frustrated with the magazine loading position, then she got it. It loaded with a click and with the cocking of the rifle - she had secured her own fate.
I would've aimed low if I'd had a better weapon, but I had to go for the torso at that distance and with a pistol. One shot did it - she dropped straight away - her long, dark hair following her body to the ground.

TUESDAY 3 NOV

I found myself standing in the aisle of the darkened Market Hall. It was all closed up of course. After unlocking the doors to my workshop, I opened my large brown leather messenger bag. The cash was in a hidden draw deep inside the messy workspace.
Some of the notes, no longer in circulation but still bankable or changeable to Euros, one post office at a time. There was much more cash than I'd remembered. I had to shove two packets - of five separate bound wads - into my raincoat pockets, as I couldn't fit any more into the sizable bag.
A small red light caught my attention - it was the answer machine telling me I had a message. A couple of customers hadn't collected their frames yet from before the lockdown - and they wouldn't be doing so from me either. Time for me to go. What strange goings on there'll be at the Market Hall over the next few days, once the lockdown is lifted. All active traders dead - and one missing.

The flashing light was irritating me, also I thought I'd have a listen for old times' sake. The message wasn't from a customer, it was a voice from beyond the grave - or so I thought. Callahan was, after all inapt at using equipment he was unaccustomed to. Bloody idiot, I thought. He wasn't assassinated, he was turned around by the Police half a mile from my safe-house and instead of saying he was returning there - he said he lived a Michael's Town, so they sent him back. He had arrived back in town at 16:00 - couldn't get to grips with the burner phone, so left the message on the answer phone from the flat - of all places. Bloody idiot! My punishment for his over confidence and incompetence, was to leave him to it, after all he and his family were safe now anyway.

I found myself having to put all thoughts that my voodoo colleagues needn't have died, out of my mind. That somehow a compromise could have been arranged.

What's done is done - no regrets.

I ran my fingers along the carved sign of my workshop as a goodbye gesture, picked up the heavy bag and left.

The streets were eerily quiet, even for lockdown. It was uncomfortable. The strange atmosphere suddenly made no sense to me. Or was it me - had my transition into someone else begun? Someone I didn't know yet. I was used to being anonymous, just another face in the crowd, an ordinary Joe, but now I was the only body on the street. Sticking out a mile with my large leather bag full to bursting point with cash.

The sun came out as I reached the promenade. It illuminated the droplets of water left from the numerous downpours that day, creating extra orange coloured seasonal lights on windowsills,

gutters and hanging from the belly of the thickly painted railings that stretched the length of the prom. Despite the sun - it felt like the end of time. The current environment could be a metaphor for my life. Dark one minute, then blades of light shining through the clouds the next. I was still determined to make this the beginning of the rest of mine.
There it was the black and grey shark-like motorhome. 'They can have what's in my coat pockets,' I thought - but then they've seen my face, interacted with me. Can there be another two casualties in this? Can I do it - just one more time? I'd been observing the old couple, on and off, for the past few weeks. It was accidental really as I was mostly admiring the wagon. Dirty bastard, the bloke though. He'd get up and out early and drag the, what I can only assume was the mini cesspit, down onto the beach, then empty the thick blue contents into the sea. That's no reason to die though - is it?
And why, all of a sudden, did I need a reason at all? My oil spill into the Ambarnaya river had been a damn sight more damaging to the environment than some geriatric liquid waste.

    As I drove out of the town that I'd grown to love, the lump in my chest felt like the unchewed piece of apple again, waiting to go down to my stomach or get regurgitated back up into my throat. I pulled over to change the ownership details using Omar's software on the laptop, and decided to write this blog, which has now taken me over eight hours to write.

The radio speaks as I finish, and morning arrives. I rub my stiff neck and painful elbow as I listen.

'Belgian scientists have announced a breakthrough in the search for a vaccine to combat Covid-19. A spokesperson announced that 'It's early days yet, but if the Coronavirus Vaccine performs as well as expected in preliminary trials, it will soon be pushed through to the last test stages. If results continue to be positive and the vaccine is passed fit for use, we could see the first vaccinations administered as soon as the early months of the new year.

In other news. A married couple, both in their late seventies were found dead, leaning against each other on a freezing bench located on the promenade at Michael's Town, near Liberty. Their bodies were discovered just after midnight. A photographer had taken a picture of fireworks going off from the beach with the couple silhouetted in the foreground. After some time, they showed no signs of movement, so she investigated and found that they had both what appeared to be self-inflicted fatal wounds. The Police have commented on the double tragedy, stating that they have no reason to suspect foul play.'
I look down at my hands as I turn the radio off. They look dirty. Like I've been digging something up, as a dog would. A combination of slight arthritic crippling, wear and tear and the heavy contrast of morning light make them look so old.
    'Goodbye Victor.' I say it out loud to make it official as I start up the engine of the shark mobile. The low, blinding winter sun was coming up and 2020 was soon to end,
'And a happy new year - who ever I'm about to become.'

END OF BLOG: 08:36
Tuesday, 3 November 2020 (GMT)

END

SHORT STORIES: By Richard Ireland.

ABOUT THE AUTHOR

PERSONAL:
Richard Ireland was born in 76', has held a copious amount of jobs as well as some military experience. He achieved a Degree in Media & Communications at the age of 20 and married his wife, Jacqui, the year after. They have three grown-up children and live in the mid-wales, coastal town of Aberystwyth.

CREATIVE:
Ireland has produced several Radio Plays and independent Film projects and has participated in other productions as sound engineer, actor, animator, videographer and photographer. He has worked in various technical positions, both as a volunteer and professionally in the Theatre. Was head designer for branding with a Tobacco company whilst working as photographic adviser for six years, and has his paintings excepted for exhibition on a yearly basis. Writing is next.